CRANNÓG MEDIA

CRANNÓG 43 autumn 2016

Editorial Board

Sandra Bunting
Ger Burke
Jarlath Fahy
Tony O'Dwyer

ISSN 1649-4865
ISBN 978-1-907017-44-5

Cover image: 'Bardic Shield' by Miles Lowry
Cover image sourced by Sandra Bunting
Cover design by Wordsonthestreet
Published by Wordsonthestreet for Crannóg magazine
www.wordsonthestreet.com   @wordsstreet

CONTENTS

The Galway Study Centre

Since 1983, the Galway Study Centre has been dedicating itself to giving an excellent education service to post-primary school students in Galway.

info@galwaystudycentre.ie
Tel: 091-564254

www.galwaystudycentre.ie

Submissions for Crannóg 44 open Nov 1st until Nov 30th
Publication date is Feb 24th 2017

Crannóg is published three times a year in spring, summer and autumn.

Submission Times: Month of November for spring issue. Month of March for summer issue.

Month of July for autumn issue.

We will <u>not read</u> submissions sent outside these times.

POETRY: Send no more than three poems. Each poem should be under 50 lines.

PROSE: Send one story. Stories should be under 2,000 words.

We do not accept postal submissions.

*When emailing your submission we require **three** things:*

1. *The text of your submission included both in body of email and as a Word attachment (this is to ensure correct layout. We may, however, change your layout to suit our publication).*

2. *A brief bio in the third person. Include this both in body and in attachment.*

3. *A postal address for contributor's copy in the event of publication.*

To learn more about Crannóg Magazine, or purchase copies of the current issue, log on to our website:

www.crannogmagazine.com

FROM HERE, I WHISPER, ANSEO   EAMONN WALL

1.
His give lessening on earth, father revolved
best amongst women, his forms adhering
to their voices, their elegance while
walking through opened doors speaking
to him of paradise. Today, continent away,
seated on sand and stone, I look east-
ward to imagine him, my dear old man,
sun-burned, his towel, togs, ear-plugs,
glasses, arms reached out better to absorb
late ounces of the sun, all that was offered,
his back was to water, eyes open to land and sky.
2.
Outside by the open back door seated our
women absorb length of evening: each holds
a cup and cigarette, the benches painted
white and blue, children now lighted out
across lane and meadow, fled like gazelles.
As I await a bus in Albuquerque, mother's
voice pings off purple sage and piñon pine.
Again, it's evening time in Co. Wexford.
Anseo, I whisper, once or twice, onto desert
air. A kite-like word can catch fire, ascend
to weigh suspended, bright immigrant star.

BY DECREE   ANNE TANNAM

I will not allow accidents in my kingdom.
In my kingdom there will be no talk of what might have been
prevented.

The word heartbroken I banish for a thousand years.
I banish messengers bringing news that breaks the heart.

There will be no blame in my kingdom.
In my kingdom no one will point the finger, no one will lay fault.

Sleeplessness will not take hold of the nighttime.
Nighttime will be free of the slow ticking clock.

Bodies laid out decades before their time, I forbid.
I forbid the stillness that gathers around the bodies.

I will not allow the aftermath to live in my kingdom.
In my kingdom the aftermath will not lay waste to the seasons.

RAPPROCHEMENT   STEVE WADE

I awake to Flynn's voice.

'Mom, Salem is outside. I heard him. I don't want to die.'

Standing before my bed, Flynn. With my senses heightened and Flynn's talk of death, he appears in the subdued light like some demon child.

'You're not going to die,' I say. 'It's another dog. Salem's gone. He's never coming back.'

Flynn's face crumples. 'But Mom, I'm really scared. Can I sleep in your room tonight?'

'Sorry love,' I say. 'Of course you can.' I pull the duvet aside. He jumps in.

Wide-awake now, neither of us is able to return to sleep. He asks me to tell him about Salem.

'But you know all about him. You've heard the stories a million times.'

'Please Mom, please.'

I know I shouldn't, but I relent.

Flynn snuggles in to me. I then tell him, as I've told him before, about Salem, the butcher's big black Labrador.

Given the freedom to wander about the village, Salem possessed an uncanny ability. When someone was gravely ill, while family members gathered round the bedside, Salem arrived on their doorstep. And he'd begin his howling, wandering off from time to time in an agitated manner, and returning at intervals, as though at the behest of some demonic summoning. Not until the afflicted man or woman passed, did Salem trot away.

Hardly have I begun a particular story about the dog, when Flynn is asleep. My own sleep, for what's left of the night, is ragged.

Before he leaves for school the next day, I tell Flynn I probably won't make it in the afternoon.

But there I am. I surprise him by turning up to collect him when he gets out. I've left work early after all.

He seems to sense my presence before he spots me. He bounds across the yard, his schoolbag jumping excitedly on his back. Both of us ignore the name-calling and the taunts aimed at him from two separate groups of kids.

We avoid the androgynous Lollipop man, a woman, in her yellow coat at the gate. Instead, we choose to cross the road at the pedestrian lights a half a minute's walk away.

Leaning down to hear Flynn above the jackhammer being worked by a man in a hard yellow hat next to a few others with shovels and picks, the uplifting lemony scent, a memory of the shampoo I lathered into Flynn's soft brown hair the night before, gives me an instant infusion of pure joy. Joy that the weekend is here and he is free for two days from the jeering, the teasing and the bullying. Joy at the first real day of spring sunshine, of the daffodils that wave cheerily from the grass verges on either side of the pedestrian island.

Then, from behind the workmen's parked lorry, roars a white car, its impatient snarl and high-pitched screech killing the thumping jackhammer.

Although that moment, a moment that will sunder everything we have ever been as mother and son, a moment that will deny all the potential togetherness left to us, lasts only seconds, I will see it always as clearly as though it were freeze-framed and I've watched it a billion times.

Before the car slams into us, the driver's teenage face is clenched: muscles bunched-up under incredulous eyes, taut skin stretched by a grinning mouth that isn't a grin; bared, snarling teeth in a face that strives to pull back the now unstoppable, freewheeling tonne of metal that detaches Flynn's hand from mine.

Shrouded in an instant, blinding whiteness, the sickening crunch of metal impacting with flesh and bone, Flynn's and mine, the intolerable pain, for me, is deadened by what I will come to realise are bodily released chemicals induced by shock. The blinding whiteness gives way to a red veil that pours from my skull.

Flynn. I have to see him, to find him, to touch him, to hold him in my arms and ensure him that everything will be okay. In my head I call out his name, but nothing comes from my mouth. I try to work my hands to my eyes to clear away the warm, sticky wetness, but my hands, like my speechless voice, are dumb, useless things that do not respond.

And then all is emptiness, nothingness. But into the void splinters snatches of a wailing ambulance siren: authoritative male voices. Misshapen words dripping into my ear. Professional hands checking, assessing and calculating.

About my body I feel tightness, as the straps on the stretcher into which I can imagine I've been carefully placed are secured. And still my eyes will not open.

But open they do, a mere flicker, enough to take in Flynn being loaded into a different ambulance by a bunch of men in green uniforms. Unable to re-open my eyes, the drumming inside my chest increases until the images dissipate, leaving me confused and disorientated.

When next I awake, Flynn is gone from me forever. Destined to move in another dimension, a cold and hostile place to which I have no access.

Impossible to fathom, unbearable to consider, I will never again hear his voice calling out 'Mom', as he so often did those Friday afternoons I left work early and surprised him in the schoolyard. Nor will I feel his vital warmth on my lips when I kiss him goodnight. Our overnight stays together in his granny's, my mother's, finished. No more walks by the canal where old men with old dogs greeted us as they would their own. The only ones who seemed to accept that Flynn and I were each other's family. Unlike the cruel, taunting schoolyard voices, like a pack of hounds, yipping and yapping hungrily at the boy with no daddy. Gone, too, the happy Sunday afternoon outings to the zoo and the seaside, the songs we sang together on the car drive now like plaintive, far-off melodies carried on the wind from another town.

The scream I scream when first I stand before that headstone in the desolate graveyard is ignored by the only living creatures present – the black-feathered fiends cackling their deep-bass caws from a band of cypress trees. I scream again, throwing back my head to beseech something, anything. But even the warming sun mocks my loss, and climbs higher into a sky, kingfisher blue.

Revenge. Never in my life have I been the vengeful sort, but hatred burns in me hotly. If reaching Flynn is impossible, I will seek out and hunt down the boy racer, as they called him, who has annihilated both our lives. Though how exactly I will carry out my vengeance I have yet to consider.

In the meantime, I get myself to all those places where Flynn's piping voice and happy laughter were once free to ring out, unaffected by the prospect of bullying classmates: The seaside with the little inlet we called *our beach*, where, sheltered from the wind, we built sandcastles and had picnics, enjoying the scrambled egg sandwiches and almond cake we made together back home. Alone, I push along the canal banks, tentatively saying 'Hello' to the old men exercising themselves and their dogs. But, without Flynn by my side, they ignore me. Except one or two dogs, whose hackles bunch and gums peel back in warning. So, on I go. I visit

Flynn's favourite, the zoo. Though my visit proves equally futile. The gorillas and the chimps, from behind their glass barriers, hardly look my way. And when they occasionally do glance in my direction, their intelligent eyes seem bursting with wistfulness. As though they know.

Finally, I overcome the fear that has kept me away too long from confronting the horror.

Past the manly lollipop woman I walk, regarding her peripherally, her mannish tones, as she carries on a laughing conversation with herself, curdling my stomach. And then, up ahead, I see him. Lying in the road at the pedestrian crossing where the accident happened over a month ago. The young man lies facedown with his hands clamped to the sides of his bleeding head, his body writhing.

An instant rage I didn't expect engulfs me. In less than an eye-blink I'm standing over him. 'Hey,' I say. 'Hey you.'

The young man's body freezes, before he pushes himself into a seated position. Younger than I recall, he stares at me and shakes his head, tears sliding over and glistening against congealed blood darker than the deepest wine.

'No,' he says. 'Please, I want me ma. Me ma is expecting me. I have to go home.'

The youth becomes hysterical then, calling out for his mother, as though she might yet come. And the way his head shunts about in all directions reminds me of how I used to find Flynn those nights not long after his daddy left us. In a trance he'd be, his eyes fully open, when I'd rush in to his room late in the night. 'I'm here, love,' I'd say. 'Mommy's here.' And for a moment Flynn's eyes would right themselves and stare at me. 'Not you,' he'd say. 'I want my real mommy.' But this was something that lasted only a couple of years.

Confused momentarily by the memories and by the moment, I imagine I hear Flynn's voice shifting on the wind. And there are other voices, too, women's voices, one that sounds like my mother.

'Ma,' the young man shouts. 'Ma.' And he works himself to his feet, his expectant face looking up the road behind me towards the school.

I turn round. Coming our way is Flynn, who pushes his granny's wheelchair. Next to them, with them, a woman I've never seen: the young man's mother.

'Ma,' the young man calls. 'I'm here, Ma.'

'They can't hear you, love,' I say. 'They can't hear us.'

For a while the youth goes on shouting for his mother, but eventually the frown on his forehead smooths, and his tears become intermittent.

I calm him further, reassuring him that even though she can neither see nor hear him, he can be with her always.

As Flynn, his granny, and the young man's mother reach us, the three speak in quieter tones. We listen.

They all three bless themselves. And then Flynn's granny, my mam, calls the young man's mother by name, and tells her how good she is for helping to look after Flynn. And how impossible it would be if she had to do things on her own. The young man's mother compresses her lips and shakes her head. Sure isn't it the least she can do, and nothing less than a pleasure to do so, she tells her. 'And God save and protect us all', she adds.

Stepping away from his granny's wheelchair, Flynn limps the few steps to a small plaque fixed to a garden wall and kisses the miniature portrait inset above the writing. 'I love you, Mommy', he says.

'I love you too, sweetheart', I say, and blow a kiss his way.

'That's a good lad', the young man's mother says, and she takes Flynn's hand in hers and helps him back to his granny's wheelchair. 'Let's go home.'

I smile at the young man who is now seated with his back to the garden wall.

Whimpering a little, he says, 'I'm sorry. I'm real sorry.'

I hold out my hand to him. He takes it, and pushes to his feet.

'It's okay', I say. 'We can go home now too.'

In an instant, we're in the cemetery, surrounded by the scattered cypresses, the yew thicket and the stand of mature oaks. The frosty air thick with the uplifting smell of wet earth and darkness, which shifts to the miasma of decaying flesh. A murder of hooded crows cackles from a lone oak tree. And overhead, a raven, his plumage as black as Salem's coat, crows a deep, guttural croak.

CURVATURE

MICHAEL C SMITH

Up-canyon abruptly
narrows and turns,

the cliffed-out slick rock wall
dwarfing the years I measure.

Glistening specks tumble by
in the feral stream's current.

Curvature walks me around
a grove of pines aching

for summer's short sunlight,
a lone wild cherry a handful

of days from bloom.
What can I know,

last season's pinecones
and the years' before strewn

like confetti across the faint
trail? The ground answers

in footprints a grazing
cow passed this way,

her faith in thick,
sweet grass growing

somewhere round
a bend somewhere ahead.

THE PLEASURE IT GIVES US   KNUTE SKINNER

We heard it before.
The obvious question is whether
it was worth hearing.

It was on yesterday's news –
Morning Ireland, *The One O'Clock News* and *Drivetime*.
It was in the *Irish Independent*
and would, no doubt, appear later
in *The Irish Times*.

The postman mentioned it,
an uneasy smile on the edge
of his earnest eyes.
Women blocking the aisles at SuperValu
were telling one another about it,
each trying to get in the first word
while nodding her grey head
in a driblet of disapproval.

And today we are hearing it again
On *Morning Ireland*
and, sure enough, it is now in *The Irish Times*.
The good effect is the pleasure it gives us all,
even as we shake our sage heads.
It's such a pity that none of it ever,
ever did occur.

THE GEOMETRY OF AUKS   MICHAEL SHARP

Hard-fisted by salt,
The wake of ships,
A shag-cry of islands,
Cormorants' rock,

A stampede of nags
Foaling like stallions
In a blizzard of surf,
A hanged man of clouds,

Jagged, bare-knuckle,
Shroud-white, obscure,
A murmur of petrels
As circular as time,

An insular Sahara
Of clock and season,
The geometry of auks
In triangular flight.

SMOKE   C. R. RESETARITS

1923

JANUARY

The bars across my heart are clear like water, stiff like steel. Bind me, confine me. Why not try the gag? At least that might give me something to chew upon. Instead, I pace my cell and rage in pantomime not to disturb my jailer's sleep.

You sent him away. Did you dispatch his memory too? I shouldn't mind if you stole mine, or quite lost your own. But you won't, right up until the end, I'm sure.

I may welcome your demise – might serve you right and me better, although once I loved you best. Do you remember, horrid papa? It was my way, in spite of you – your warts and worries, your ill will. I'd like another way now. I had another until you interceded on your own behalf, until you interfered.

At night I try to dream of him and me and our time, when I was who I *really* am. But I never dream that. No, I dream I'm caught in a small room up a dark tower, near the sea. From my window I contemplate the rhythm of water, analyse the life it holds and sanctifies. Lofty thoughts but awfully high and dry. I'd rather feel than think, rather sink than rise above. I needn't understand the tides to enjoy their threat. Better wet than dry. Better me than you.

Yes, all right. I know all the doors are open. There is no steel between us, only our own fire-forged, iron wills. I long to escape, run away, and I do feel I'm meant to, but, shhhh, just this moment, I see how you've weakened and I'm afraid.

MARCH

True bindings around my limbs, organs, thoughts. Sitting at our door, open to winter, I see only high rock walls and hedges of steel. And all because you felt the need to send my love away and then go yourself, a decades-long exit, but I find I can't hate you as I did once, would rather now. And while I know the bindings and the steeled green are my invention, mine alone, mine to cast or keep, there is yet between us our fire-forged longing. Yours, mine. Even in death. Especially, in death, we are so alike, papa, and I know you'd admire my tumbling full speed into the lane – but as your casket moves past the garden gate, I'm rather bound up and can't yet find my way for steel and tears.

MAY

And so I'm free. Free and drifting upon a world of roll and water, a world whose motion is bound by lunacy, and rightly so. I watch the islands grow at dawn, bigger and bigger, and the seabirds circling above, smaller and smaller. I wave and feel as if I might be waving at shimmering bits of my own circling soul. Once while sneaking into hospital circling the beds in dim light, my body shrank to the size of my lover's palm, the gap between his lips. Mysteries at night, in moonlight through a leaded window.

I loved him when a soldier, when a beautifully injured soldier, and I stole kisses when he was asleep. Soon he will be my husband and at night we will both sneak and thief.

JUNE

I once imagined love to be like that, magic shrinkings in moonlight or hovering souls, eternal mates, bodies transformed, rattleback tops seeking their perfected spin, but no. All the poets promised better. Even your Mr Walt Whitman and his ever-rocking, twosome sea,

'Delaying not, hurrying not,

Whisper'd me through the night . . .'

But really, is this then everything? I thought freedom more dear than dull. Oh I'm sure it's wondrous and I will grow into these new habits as a young buck does new velvet. I do feel differently about . . . well, I'm sure, a great many things although nothing much that matters. Except the journey, travelling. And I quite love the sound of the sea and you again in spite of all

I thought was done and dead and gone.

AUGUST

We stand before the Lion Gates of Mycenae, dusty home of kings, where you and he found fortune, fame. An odd honeymoon. Endlessly, the endlessness of tide and time. He has little time but great tides and a strong undertow: he hunts me up after a long blank day, after the evening's wine and food, after the old friends chatting through antiquity. Later in our room he approaches smiling – though not always smiling – and I feel his body-being tug at the back of my legs, and deep into waves I go. How kind of Nature to make finite duty but not the lovely tides.

OCTOBER

'There is the railway to Mecca,' his assistant Tommy informs. 'This is just the place where Lawrence kept rail cutting to stop the Turks.'

I remember T. E. racing his old motorbike down the lane behind our house and then, of course, he gave me his condolences at your funeral and wake. I wonder how that shy, small man was so transformed by what seems from above such a pale, shifting, land. How – oh, please, please – shall I? I'd love nothing quite so much as derailing a few Turks myself.

The world spins outside my window.

He is working at numbers two seats up. Our plane declining now and everyone for a moment inclining. Tommy next to me smiles and directs me out the small window as odd white structures go whizzing by. What do you think, I whisper. What indeed, Tommy hums. Square sheep, grave markers, blurred brides?

Tommy and I in secret laughing.

The sun is setting behind us. I can see the curving Euphrates. Shacks, more railway lines, the Tigris. We angle out, tight smooth arc. I see we are very low gliding over land, jolt and bounce. You should see your face, Tommy says. We disembark onto an open field. The short, dry grasses rustle, hum. In the distance, dogs are baying. The wind is warm and gentle. I breathe deeply, am newly me again.

DECEMBER

In the still darkness of our bed he asks why I didn't tell him that Tommy and I were leaving to go to market, then to town. Tommy said I should go and so. But I don't tell him that, I say, errands for cook, for fitting in. I say, as you asked of me, dear. And he's silent, but not asleep. Perhaps I've disturbed his finely wrought sensibilities. He's all him, his work, his fame, his others. He says I should learn a task to help me better fit his life. Fit, indeed. Tommy says I'm fit – perfectly fit for that matter – just as I am and meanwhile the world, up close, is really a carnival of scraps and tatters, like the yarn balls our kittens used to love to pounce and battle. Pretty in spin, petty in hand. Remember? Funny, I suppose. Or sad.

1924

JANUARY

I think I will burn this journal. Smoke might prove a better way to reach you and evade *him*. What has became of my lovely hurt soldier, whose smile was spring morning and summer midnight?

You were right about him, papa. However did you know? And how, please, do I proceed?

I risked everything to steal his kisses long ago in hospital, scaling vines and lattice to slip through barely opening windows in the dead of night. I feel I risk nothing much in stealing injuries or planting beautiful, dark kisses on a face even younger than my own. Everything or nothing or something obscure and in-between, like fog or smoke or secrets once again. How to proceed once I see it wasn't him I loved but, perhaps, the haze of secrets, of climbing forbidden walls, slipping in night-sky windows, my dearest, dearest papa?

I THINK IT A PITY TO EAT LARKS' TONGUES
ROSEMARIE ROWLEY

I think it a pity to eat larks' tongues
Even the velvet tongue of the calf
Does not utter images to test the brain

With gold of antiquity
Or lust's revenge
But must be comestible with fact.

But larks' tongues!
I cannot reproach the lioness
For jealousy of her cub

But he or she who pulled out
The root of song
And placed it in my mouth

Has surely a jealous heart
And is a bearer of news
And views far
From the vaulted
Heaven of your song
Who can eat that fare –
Someone who hasn't a
Note of your music.

DAEDALUS SPEAKS TO ICARUS, HIS SON   LIZ QUIRKE

How it is that I who can coax stone
into labyrinthine detail could fail
to build the basics of your senses?

My greatest success stands as a reliquary
to forever keep what little was gathered of you,
your robe, splinters of your bones,

slivers of pride among scattered, waxless feathers,
fingertips still reaching towards the sky.

My son, you surrendered to the vanity
of a daring death, tested yourself
in elemental ways you were not born to conquer.

No Apollo you, what was your last thought?
Did you call Father into the wind as you fell?

Or did the arrogance that the next upward gust was yours
keep you silent as the water rushed to fill your mouth?

The women say their mothering ears still hear your cries,
their night-feed hearts slowed to a dimming thrum

when you failed to breach the surface.
They detailed in that way of women
how it feels to see a child's body broken,

because you were child to them,
and they can cry for you and remember
your newborn skull warm in the palm of their hand.

WEEKEND IN LONDON   AOIBHEANN MCCANN

John realises at that moment that he's only ever scratched the surface of Triona in the past year because when he asks her who the guy was who smiled at her in The Tate when they were looking at Ophelia, she tells him to fuck off.

Later, because he refuses to speak to her, she says she did know the attendant; he was a friend of Tariq's, a guy she went out with. He is excited that she is being open, so he asks her what Tariq was like; she says he DJed in a club called The Gas Club in Battersea. She tries to leave it at that, going into the tiny bathroom so the fan goes on and there is a barrier of sound and a door between them. So John looks it up on his tablet, he finds a Gas Club in Leicester Square. Then he googles DJ Tariq, he looks at the images. They are mostly too young to be him, except one black guy with greying dreadlocks. He decides that this must be the man who made her heart impenetrable.

When Triona emerges, John tells her about The Gas Club but not about the DJ Tariq with dreadlocks; she's annoyed and says she doesn't know why John is even looking. Then she says she was never there anyway, although she was on her way there to see Tariq play one night with two girls from a tower block in Chelsea. She says they took speed from a wrap made out of a trashy women's magazine, a 'My-boyfriend-slept-with-the-best-man-on-our-wedding-night' type of one. The girls from Chelsea were sisters; one of them was called Charlotte, either the fat one or the thin one. They worked on the newspaper kiosk near the pub she worked in. It's bullshit, Triona says, about not knowing anyone in London; she knew loads of people when she lived here. Anyway, maybe they went towards Battersea that night, she doesn't remember, she just remembers taking a wrap of speed in the toilets of a pub with the thin one. The thin one was always miserable, something bad had happened to her, man-related probably. The paper stall belonged to their dad, and Triona didn't think he was very nice; maybe he abused them or something. Triona says she never usually took speed, preferred to get Ecstasy or weed from fat Billy who lived around the back of her sister's.

John has never even been to London before, a fact Triona finds ridiculous. Everyone in Ireland lived in London in the nineties she says, more Irish in the UK than in Ireland. Just a few redheads left at home to haul a few bags of turf on a donkey to give the Yanks something to take a picture of.

Anyway she never got to the Gas Club that she remembers, maybe it was actually in Leicester Square she says and anyway Tariq stopped calling to her after that. She says she never knew where he lived but she went up to his friend Ray's flat once, when she was really drunk, stalker style. She says she had been smoking weed and watching cricket, she says she felt slow and green all over, inside and outside.

John met Triona at work, at the sports and social club. They went bowling. She says her mother would love him, John can't imagine why. John knows his own mother would hate her because Triona is twice his age, educated, blonde and wears suits. His mother has never met any of his girlfriends, John thinks she's given up hope; she's already invested in the boys from his class, the ones in the estate anyway, the ones she wanted him to get away from, the ones who weren't clever enough to get out of the area or were maybe pretending not to be so they didn't have to. His mother gives their kids sweets and lends their wives teabags.

'So what's the craic in Dublin?' they say when they see him.

'Same old,' John says.

'Jesus, hi, you've got the accent now,' they say.

He knows they'd fancy Triona, just because they didn't go to school with her. John remembers their wives names from school; they were all younger than them.

Though you'd never think it, Triona is from a small town on the border too, but further south, Monaghan. She went to college in London because there were no fees and Triona's parents wouldn't have got a grant. She worked in bars and that was why her accent is flat, hammered down by years of misinterpretation. It's all snippets with Triona, she rarely elaborates like this, on her life, usually changes the subject when John probes for more, like she's still working in a bar and he's the alcoholic at the end of the counter she has to humour.

He puts down the tablet that he has been holding to his chest like a shield and reaches for her. She pushes him away though they haven't had sex since they arrived. He reckons she's turned off because the hotel is shit, more like a homeless hostel than the boutique steal he was hoping for. There is an awning on the front door that looked good on the web but up close it is bent and dusty and clearly hadn't been fully folded out since they took the picture. It is navy and says 'Promenade' on it in white cursive script.

She opens the window and is standing looking down at the roar of traffic through the grimy sash windows. John cannot believe how overwhelmingly dirty London is; when he showered earlier the water turned black. She announces she has something to show him. John is curious as he follows her out the door of the hotel and towards the river. He thinks they are going back to the Tate, he imagines her confronting the gallery attendant who smiled at her about Tariq, about the way he looked her up and down in front of John, but then she crosses the road at a flashing orange light and he nearly gets run over by a black cab. They stop outside a pub called The Princess Royal, it is near Buckingham Palace; when they go in it is quiet in a way that only English pubs can be. By the window there are two men playing giant Jenga and another one on the fruit machines.

'It hasn't changed at all', she says.

'Did you work here? You should tell the barman you worked here.'

'It's weird without the smoke', she sighs, and stares at the barman polishing glasses.

'Did you used to smoke?'

She doesn't answer.

He is hungry now but there is nothing here she will eat, there is only fried fatty food on the chalkboard. He orders drinks.

'Let's sit outside', she says.

He follows Triona out to the beer garden. It is a concrete yard with a few tables and some patio heaters. There is a man with a white pit bull who resembles him on a leash; the man is drinking a pint of bitter from a glass tankard. As they sit down he downs the rest and leaves, yanking the dog away from them as it rears up.

'So is the beer garden the same?' John asks.

She rolls her eyes for an answer. Her eyes look far away now, glazed.

In the office where they work she is a manager in another department, much higher up than him, so they keep their relationship to themselves. Triona says it's better that way, says she could get into trouble, or that he could be passed over for promotion. He has pointed out that Andy and Sarah seem to manage. John feels like a cliché, like someone who should write to an agony aunt and have the problem resolved in the Sunday paper, but Ireland is too small, he is afraid everyone will know it is him. His friends are all agony aunts these days anyway.

Telling him to dump her. But he knows he could get to the core of Triona, the place that he finds sometimes when she's half asleep after sex, or first thing in the morning when she is soft and semiconscious, or when she is hungover, though to be hungover she has to be drunk first and wants to have sex that is angry and mechanical, both of them chugging to the top of that hill, laboured in third gear, numb with drink but determined. John thinks he loves her and wonders if she would soften if they lived together or if they could be open about their relationship in work. He wants to reach in through her chest and pull out that unhappy part, that bitterness, that edge of nastiness and rip it out like an Evangelist preacher and show it to her, black and pulsating, and then throw it away, as someone shouts Halleluiah. But instead, he goes in and gets another pint for himself and a gin and tonic for her;; he gulps half the pint down at the bar. She must know he is going to say something serious as she starts talking and talking when he puts the drink in front of her, asks him did he see an Irish note over the bar. She says when she worked here she put one there, it stopped the bar being blown up, she says, that was the code then, she says; her Northern accent got her into trouble sometimes, laid her bare to the customers who wanted to have a go at her about the IRA.

'Did you ever think of marrying this Tariq guy?' John interrupts.

She snorts. 'What? Seriously? It was just a fling, he had another girlfriend, for God's sake.'

'I think I'm going to stay here.' John says.

She turns in her seat, her eyes wide, scruntinising him.

'In the pub?' she asks.

'No, in London.' John hasn't thought this through but gets carried away, suddenly wanting to liven this pub up.

He jumps up and runs back into the bar. 'Champagne!' John says, thumping the counter.

'We've got Babycham.' The barman's monotonous voice threatens to change John's mind, but he thinks of the people he will meet and the stories he will have too when he returns someday.

'Babycham it is.'

She looks subdued when John comes back with the two small bottles and two wine glasses.

'Are you serious about all this?' she asks.

'Yes!' John says, because now John is, 'Let's stay here, get jobs, start anew! I'll never understand you unless I live here, I'll never have any stories to tell you.'

'Don't be ridiculous, people only move here when they don't have jobs. We have jobs,' she says.

'Oh,' he says. He hadn't thought of that.

'What about your flatmates? Not fair to them really. That's another thing, it's very expensive here, you'll never afford a place to live. And I don't know if you'll even get a reference if you leave like this.'

'Maybe I'll live here,' he says.

'You're allergic to dogs.'

He doesn't understand, is she talking about the white pit bull? She does not mention their relationship. They finish their Babycham and leave.

Back at the hotel he goes first to the reception, rings for the girl and asks her about vacancies as Triona mounts the dusty narrow stairs to their room.

The next day he walks her to Victoria Station, walks her to the barriers of the tube. She gets a ticket from the machine, and yanks her suitcase through and doesn't look back.

He walks back to the hotel, confident. The room is darker now, shadowed by Monday morning. He looks out at the traffic. He runs his finger through the grime in the window and draws a heart.

WILD CHIVE   MATT PRATER

As elders used vinegar and honey,
I use wild chive to bless the year.
It needs no sweetened mitigation,
its own green burn a compliment
to the ground it lights from, and sedge
its little bundles mirror and usurp.
After the crocuses' announcements;
after the white drops of galanthus
tender their bells; after the Shrove,
here come bitters to break the fast.
It is garlic and onion and grass all,
the green spit of God's good bitter.
Whoever says it hurts their stomach
must live on milk, because I've known
no cleaner taste than that cold cord,
which I twist and bend against itself
to gnaw at the cold knot, to stain
my breath and unrender the winter.

SUMMER NATURE NOTES   MARY O'DONNELL

1.
Bees in the Laburnum

For days, they have been humming,
buried in each blossom, thrusting in, out,
in again, the world's wide thighs so welcoming,
golden, scent of pollen maddening the lust
for duty in such a droop-dipped sky-hive,
those drips of light and aurulence,
open invitations to suck and sweeten,
drawing out till sacs swell,
wings are musked
and hanging dells of flower
stop trembling only at dusk.

2.
Grey Crows

They hate the little dog
about her business in the garden.
Defensive of hatchlings
within the beech, they screech
and trail her to the forest edge,
occasionally swoop across her path.
Nose down, ears pricked, she ignores them;
even so, they hurl and ooze murder,
primeval to the last,
pale wings daubed by the fate
of being so grey, so in-between
black crow and raven. Being neither,
with much to defend, these beaks

are weapons, not for snail shells,
but for splitting small skulls,
razoring soft belly, ripping innards,
the sweetest, thick, blood-drips
to the gaping mouths of chicks.

3.
The Storm

Not as violent as predicted, but even so,
memories are long, and storms have
rent the crop-bulged fields in vicious mosaics
of hurricane prints, flattening that ochre,
those stiff, sky-pricking tips
to a brown, matt ooze.
Just before, the birds stop singing, wind drops
then gathers in a rush of violent skirt,
flings itself across the north of the county,
lightning skewered from the splayed fingers
of an old god who reminds us, yet again,
that we are but feckless fools
who watch the still, refracted light,
in thrall to rainbows.
Later, the sun sets in shock
on a trembling horizon,
and the moon dares show its face
over the mountains,
while the land gasps towards night
and people close their windows
against the dialect of darkness.

MEETING THE BEARDED LADY   CHERYL PEARSON

The boss man parts the curtains like he parts his hair –
with confidence and grease. *One night only!* the posters scream
in the same colour red as the silk pegged to the field
where flattened grass knows *dim* for the first time; knows *hush*.
But back here, past the sawdust circle, the hooves
are far as thunder; the sequins stars in another universe.
Here, in the quartered dark, the curtain falls behind you like water,
and your throat rehearses every swallow twice.

This is how you know she's real: the sour tang
of booze on her breath, the fur of her bangled arm. All night
she sits and soaks up looks like this, all night she stares from under
brows
that might hide wolves or bloodied children, her stiff chin eating light.
You've seen a mile of wheat do that – take sunshine down like a pint
of beer, then spill it back to gild the sky, all gold, all joy. This is the
opposite.
Nothing comes back from that midnight glare, the bib of whiskers
hung from ear to jaw and boiling with shadow. She collects your minute
there with the rest. And, when you leave, the sharp scent of your sweat.

In tens of years, a grandchild dandled from your lap will hear
how witchcraft shimmered in the tent that night like hazed heat.
Neither of you will ever know that spells and bones were as alien to her
as they were to you. That all she was thinking was if she would ever
taste, firsthand, a kiss. Whether it would be salt or sweet.

STORAGE   DAVID MORGAN O'CONNOR

You know that love I gave you? Do you mind
bringing it wherever you go? In the sea to test
salt-resistance, under that shower to lather the lava
pebbles, in the mosquito net where the hammock
swings cool and clean and turns your shin skin into
tiny square road maps, that old tough love that
fits into books and glove boxes saving lives
and time when the sea breeze blows your wet-hair
east into the future or west into maternal eruptions
like nothing we've ever seen before becoming
someone you never thought you'd be, lighter from
lifting, love is no feather to carry but I'll help
more than you think, if we can just remember where
we put the damned thing.

PETRONILLA DE MEATH   JOHN MURPHY

The flaying seconds go, as all time goes,
and going slowly on, the inches and miles go,
and so the journey to my dying breath goes,
slow, hard, and halt, its length and time go.

And the inch of time takes root in the slow miles
I have walked for days, whipped and flayed
through six godly parishes to a kindling where
the living fire is mine, and the blistering seconds

candling my breath burn centuries down inches
of miles to my last confession. Three ways I burn
yet still I live, and my slow brightness goes down
in second, breath, and inch, into Lord Ossory's fire,

to meet, like Shadrach, Meshach, and Abednego,
Death, the fourth and last, the king of fire.

AUTUMN SONATA   SIMONE MARTEL

Laura trudged up to Peter's duplex, past Mrs Chen standing in her half of the front yard among her yellow and orange flowers. In Peter's half, dandelions sprouted in cracked soil; takeout menus and free weeklies bleached and curled. While Laura waited for Peter to answer his door, she unzipped her backpack and found her dad's cheque.

All she ever saw of Peter were his hands, pale and pink-knuckled, first as they opened the door and took the cheque, then as they cleared sheet music off the piano bench and finally as they poised beside hers on the keys. 'I think he never goes outside,' she'd said. 'He's like something disgusting under a rock.' Her dad had laughed: 'He's an innocent music student trying to pay his tuition.'

'Have you ... mmm?'

'Every morning before school,' she told Peter, not mentioning that she'd practised with the TV on and an English muffin dripping butter over the piano keys. She liked to twist on the bench and work out the notes one at a time. Then she'd lick butter off her fingers and try again. A satisfactory rhythm would begin to develop and by the fourth time through, the rhythm had taken over. Now, on Friday, it was fixed, inevitable. Laura played the tune for Peter twice, with all the same mistakes.

'Again. Only this time, read the music.'

Slowly, painfully, they picked her song to pieces. After five minutes, nothing of it remained. Laura sat with her face close to the music book, her fingers clumsy, her body tense with un-learning. Outside, an ice cream truck's jingle grew louder. She wished they could go outside and buy Popsicles and talk. They'd look into each other's eyes, instead of at their hands on the piano keys. She'd show him the drawings in her art binder. Just because she was bad at piano didn't mean she was bad at everything.

Now that the ice cream truck's song had faded, they were both listening through the pinging piano notes for her father's footsteps on the porch. The sun had begun to set, the room growing orange and even dimmer. Dusk fell like a judgment, a doom: too late for this day, anyhow.

'Rats.' Laura had let loose a stream of notes – trying to get to the next line – and

33

in her rush had lapsed into the old way.

'Try again.'

Laura said goodbye to the bottom of the page and started over.

*

Dorothea Chen paused with her secateurs above her gold and rust-coloured chrysanthemums as a white BMW rolled up to the kerb. A man in a suit hurried along the walkway that ran parallel to her own, returning a minute later with the girl walking quickly at his side. The expensive car bucked away down the street, leaving silence. Soon the light would be too dim for Dorothea to continue deadheading her spent flowers. Her eyes moved to her neighbour's door. On the other side of its blank face of chipped brown paint she heard a stifled cry or scream. Then the notes began – a waterfall of music that would stop, return as a trickle, then pour forth again more forcefully. He would be at it all evening, practising, practising, as though trying to exorcise a spirit from the piano. Poor boy. And poor girl. Each week she dragged herself up to the door and flew out of the house an hour later as though a demon were after her.

Dorothea returned her secateurs to their leather holster. In the dirt border that mirrored her own, dandelions shed their fluff in the evening breeze. Dorothea's eyebrows rose toward her hairline. To share a yard with a boy who grew weeds instead of flowers crowded her as surely as sharing a piano bench for sixty minutes a week seemed to crowd those two young people. She'd been growing flowers for forty years, though, and knew that a garden was an invitation to aphids and mildew and dandelions, that success and frustration were inseparable and that, most of all, beauty was a private thing, difficult to share with anyone. She kept trying, of course, offering a view of mums to passersby on foot or car or bus, but mostly she cherished the autumnal blooms for their own sake and for herself: a worthy love, if solitary.

As the streetlamps flickered on, Dorothea turned toward her own front door, then paused again before going in, as an orange dragonfly, bright and shiny as hard candy, whirred past her ear. She turned to watch it hover over her cement birdbath and shoot out toward the road, buzzing, into the steady grind of commute traffic, flame-coloured, vanishing under the street lamps' moonlight glow.

PICTURE BOX   JAMES O'SULLIVAN

The keyboard snapped –
a decade's curation piled high and set alight –
as fat teenagers, sunburnt fools wandering far,
I watched us burn – even your reflection
in Chicago's cloud was wiped away,
your kind face in the wet snow a memory
lost to abandoned fairs on rotting slats.
The fire was contained – I still keep hold
of one picture box, where the wet cobbles
and smoky market stalls serve instead
of hollow selfies and portraits posed.
Look at how those buildings bend –
I wonder what they're like inside?
I was glad to hear you had made one home –
we dreamt so much of streets like these,
of cafés and coffeeshops – for me, smoked ribs,
and you, deep fried balls of dough – pottertjes!
I cannot look deeply at that rolling stack –
each alley swallows you with pangs of happier days
when I walked convinced that this was life now,
that we had survived the last of the northern birds.
But now, it is just me and the pigeons –
where cathedrals once stood, there is only wreckage –
'danger, demolition', it reads,
the yellow giving way to creeping brown.

WALSHPOOL LAKE   SARA MULLEN

She is an eye, this morning
as softly violet as an evening cloud.

Skyward, steadily she gazes.
I wonder if she's ever blinked,

even once, since settling here
and welling up the glen

cloven from land she carried
and pushed, her force flagging,

a broken spell, her mantle
melting into a new green era.

Life tiptoed, sidled, darted;
tasted and marked her; decided to stay.

Trees rose, held the sky up to her,
twinning them: which was which?

Men came: axed the space around her,
built an island; her hazel iris.

They harried her with spears,
jostled her with oars for the odd fish.

She took the occasional soul down
to the calcified bones she hugs to herself.

The clog of a bell: a saint came by;
made holy a neighbouring well, not her.

Monks forced pike on her.
These her teeth now, nipping bare toes.

Snatching rats and gulls, they thrive still.
Teeming, they swallow each other down.

She has blue days and sparkles. Boats
scramble down hills, beetle-legged.

Fathers row out. Then, ropes
around their waists, the kids shiver.

Inky this close, she's stern-looking.
Cold. A child might need a push.

Her edges froze one winter. They skated till she
took their dog when he dashed too far out.

Iron black, wind-mashed, she foams,
thrashes her confines, tosses the shrieking gulls.

A fallen moon blinks, wavers to her pulse
on summer nights. Maybe she dreams

of rising, stretching, gathering herself
and going some other place.

THE MEANING OF THE TIGER   CLARE MCCOTTER

after India's Daughter

There is no way to start
to write to think of you leaving the cinema
possibly pondering the meaning of the tiger
crossing an ocean with a boy on a raft
a metaphor for the dark side of the self
or just a tiger red in tooth and claw.

Child you are waiting
beneath a Munirka moon swallowed in smog
you are waiting to board that bus
one swish closes the doors, soon
the magnolia tree will turn the colour of pain
your womb full of stars
falling one by one to their death.

Child is the only word
on a tongue that knows you are woman
fighting with broken nails and broken teeth
and broken screams, eviscerating fingers
trying to hollow you to fill nothing
the gnawing nothingness in themselves.

Silently glinting in night forests
the tiger is a solitary hunter,
rank with each other's stale seed and sweat
they hunt down quarry in a pack
their grunts and squawks unable to smother
the garnet glimmering in your throat.

Others would have morphined out
the consciousness you clung to those last days
possibly pondering the meaning of man
daughter of a mother
stooping in blue snowmelt
to trace on a high crescent Himalayan lake
the contours of your face.

CROSSWORDS   NOEL KING

Deirdre is not dead. She hasn't left me. Her clothes are still here, all the creams and lotions she puts on her face. She's my wife, my best friend. Every morning I go to the hospital to see her. I talk to her. I buy *The Irish Times* and read it aloud to her. I know the bits she will like. I don't get a response; there are tubes everywhere around her body.

I go again in the evening and bring the *Evening Herald* and talk her through that. Then we stick on the telly, she has always liked *Coronation Street*, and *Fair City*. Deirdre will know the characters by their voices, of course. And she knows I'm here. I'm not a follower of the soaps myself so I lounge at the end of her bed and do the crossword; now and then I touch her hand.

I have a thing about crosswords, you see, I've been doing the one in *The Irish Times* now every day since 1973. I keep it in the newspaper until it's as complete as I can get it, then I cut it out and ease it into a plastic pocket, date it, and put it in a ring-binder. I have now started my 41st ring-binder. Each of the previous 40 are all proudly shelved in my study. When we were dating from the early to late 70s, Deirdre found it charming when she discovered my 'obsession', but later said she thought it a bit weird. She used to tell people about it, but then started to refrain from telling anyone. The dated ring-binders are there for all to see in my study; the older ones gone a bit faded now, the clasps and wiring beginning to rust; but all that work of my brain is in there, I tell you.

We fight and argue quite a lot actually. To quote the poet Sarah Robey: '...*or the faithful precision of a weekly row, / a reminder that we matter, here, now.*' That describes me and Deirdre exactly, it builds up slowly, a myriad of tiny little things and then she erupts. Sometimes, the cross words can go on into the evening right up to bedtime. But the night's sleep beside each other melts the row.

*

Last night I went to see a local amateur production of *The Weir*, Conor McPherson's seminal work from 1997. We had two tickets. I could have asked someone to take Deirdre's seat, but I went alone. This morning I decided to go through her wardrobes and wash everything, a gentle 30 degrees wash did them nicely. I want to keep everything fresh for when she gets home.

We have His & Hers bathrooms, mine on the left of the master bedroom, hers on the right. I have rarely been in hers, having no need to, while she's often in mine to take my laundry basket down to the utility room. She always cleans both bathrooms too, bless her heart.

This morning there is something puzzling me and it's not how to operate the washing machine. No, it's a question in the crossword: 13 Across. Arthur's friend in *The Hitchhikers Guide to the Galaxy* (4 letters). Dammit, I don't know. No idea. I'll look it up later. You could 'Google it' you might well say but I think that's too lazy, I prefer to extend my mind through my collection of books. When 'the Hikers' was in vogue I was teaching evening classes, Arts & Crafts, and Deirdre was an Avon lady every evening, eight years she did that for, very successful at it she was too.

*

When Deirdre and I met we were working together in a department store, and it was *she* asked *me* out. There was a local festival on and she asked if I'd like to make a date. I was shocked, there didn't seem to be anything leading up to it, no flirting or that, you know what I mean. I didn't tell my family, I had never been on a date, didn't know how to act. That night we never held hands or kissed and the both of us paid our share of everything but it was a date nevertheless. We had a certain amount of mutual respect initially, that grew into compatibility and then love. And it was love, deep love for all of the forty-three years since we met.

She loves Gay Byrne, on the radio; all the years I was out working, Gaybo was like the other man at home in the kitchen every morning. He's reached 80 now but he has a jazz programme of a Sunday. I tape it for her, recycling some old BASF cassette tapes. I found a little Walkman that's been around the house for years. Luckily it still works although the batteries had started to degrade inside; I used a tweezers to release them and cleaned it out with a baby wipe. At a local store I picked up a nice, understated, easy-wear set of headphones for her. At the hospital I place them in her ears, press play and Gaybo comes on. I imagine there is a small smile from the corner of her mouth then and I squeeze her hand.

*

Deirdre is not dead. She hasn't left me. Her clothes are still here, all the creams and lotions she puts on her face. She's my wife, my best friend. We both appeared in a bit of amateur drama over the years. I've treaded the boards since childhood but my wife only as an adult. It was a dare. A local woman, a bit of a diva really, and a snob into the bargain who looked down on Deirdre and me, was going for the lead part. I dared Deirdre to give her a run for her money and put herself up for the part. There was consternation from your wan when Dee got it, ha, ha. I must remember to recall that when I get to the hospital later. First I must do a few jobs around the house, cut the grass and get advice on how to look after the roses; the roses are Deirdre's department, must keep them looking their best for when she gets home. Oh I must remember to see if I can make a tape of her favourite album, Carole King's, *Tapestry*, from 1971. As long as I've known her she has loved that album. We have both the LP and the CD here. It would be nice if I could play it in her walkman at the hospital.

This estate was new in 1979 when we moved in, all the couples were young. The next-door neighbour on our right grew lilies and sweet peas. His wife painted still lifes and gardenscapes. Once, we went on a holiday together, the four of us, but it didn't work out really. They were a grand couple for drinks at Christmas or talking over the garden wall about Fianna Fáil and Labour and the state of the country, but to be in close proximity twenty-four hours a day was another thing altogether.

When I park and walk to the hospital front door I am always anxious, every time, there's no getting over it. I avoid the welcome smiles of the receptionist. As I press the lift open I get more anxious, impatient for it to reach the third floor where my beloved lives. Then I almost run down the corridor with its very shiny floor. But when I leave it is completely different, when I leave I feel deflated, think what am I going to cook that evening, think of how long the evening ahead is and how I'm going to fill it and who is going to ring and how hard it is to stay positive.

'Dee, I must decorate the front room before you get home. I wonder what colour you would like, love? The one we have, that grand, rich colour, magnolia, has been in our front room since 1983. Maybe you'd like a change?'

I have a packet of ginger nut biscuits in the hospital room cupboard. They were our favourites when we could share such things. I press my right index finger on the one on top of the packet and it is softening already, nothing can stop the humidity of the hospital from softening biscuits.

Last evening I fancy she peered at me, that she disapproved of something, the shirt I was wearing perhaps – it was my second day in it and I slept in it the night before. I must strive not to let my standards down, vow to be cleanshaven and spruced up every other day I ever come in here.

I was doing the crossword and was confronted with one last thing to finish it: 9 Across: The End is Nigh (5 letters). Hmm, I thought about it for ages. In cryptic puzzles either the beginning or the end of the clue defines the solution. In this case we need a five-letter word that means both END and NIGH. And the solution is CLOSE. I fill it in, fold the paper and stuff it in my trenchcoat on the back of the hospital room door.

*

Deirdre used to play the piano, purely for pleasure mind you; there was a big plan one time that she'd give up work and teach at home. Anyway, a few months back she decided enough was enough, she already had the arthritis so it was time to give up. We couldn't bear to part with the piano, who'd take it anyway, people only buy digital pianos these days. It remains centre stage in the living room. But she placed all her sheet music in the front room and instructed me to take it to a local charity shop. It was only today I got around to doing it and you'll never guess what the first book on top of the pile was – John Thompson's *Exercises for Two Hands*. I felt very sad. I stopped tears coming to my eyes.

Paperwork and clutter are mounting up, I'm getting final reminders of bills I haven't had a chance to pay with all the hospital trips, the dining room table is clutter, clutter, clutter. I must sort it soon. Last night I dreamt of Deirdre's parents and the first time I met them. I woke and found myself in the bathroom, there was breath-fog on the mirror, but I wasn't sure it was mine. I hastily looked behind me almost expecting to see a figure but of course I was alone. It, er, froze my marrow, that. It had to have been my own breath of course. I had probably pressed my face too close to the glass without realising it.

To be honest all the décor is hers, I don't know what I'll do with it after she's gone. A man can't live alone with mink and pink couches and curtains. And there isn't a crack in a wall or a creak under a floorboard that hasn't been dealt with by a carpenter or builder. We were even completely re-wired there about eight years ago. She is not dead. She hasn't left me. Her clothes are still here, all the creams and lotions she puts on her face. She is my wife, my best friend. Getting back to the crosswords, I am gathering up the ones from the past week and placing them in the 2016 ring binders. That's the very thing I'm at when the hospital phones.

NEXT OF KIN   EAMONN LYNSKEY

... see, David was the kind when things got rough
he'd always help... ... He leaves a wife and son.
She took it bad ... For all of us it's tough.
We miss him awful ... ... Can't believe he's gone.

*

Matthew was ... ... the best you'd ever find.
The army man spoke of the legacy
courageous men and women leave behind...
But losing Matthew ... It's a tragedy.

*

Our Carl was killed while clearing IEDs.
His tour was nearly up ... He was that close
to coming home ... ... and then the news he'd died.
It's hard on them out there ... and hard on us.

*

... our Kay. Our girl ... So good at everything.
There wasn't any challenge she wouldn't meet,
no matter what ... ... So when they came recruiting
she enlisted. Only there a week ...

JANICE   ADRIENNE LEAVY

The small study
        at the back of our house
is where I hung the mirror.

Copper plated, it was bought
        when the Murphys still had money
for ornamental artifacts.

This was the last item I took
        from my mother-in-law's house
before the estate sale truck arrived.

It joined several shelves filled with her books –
        mid-century American novels,
some first editions and the complete works of Shakespeare.

She left college
        to marry a doctor
in an era when women still did that.

I always keep her books in my view –
        I placed the mirror
directly across from them –

I'd have to bend down to see myself in it,
        disturbing in the process
the reflection of the opposite wall.

WALKING SARAH KELLY

It is the type of cold that seeps into your fingers
While you're too busy chatting.
The kind of darkness that could swallow
You whole if you didn't know where you were going.
It is a night that is so vast,
It almost makes you feel insignificant.
The smattering of stars
Against the absolute black
Has the power to stop
Everything else,
Just for a moment.
Headlights come at us, glowing like
Eyes, then slowing,
Illuminating the tired daffodils.

MALO CAMINO   SEÁN KENNY

Draft of letter, July 3rd

Dear Claire,

We said, didn't we, that we would keep in touch? (Despite everything.)

I have moved on. That's the truth of it. And I'm walking the Camino to prove it. (A little literal, perhaps. But there you are. Real life is not some polished metaphor, Claire. It's a messy ragged glorious thing. It is *real*.)

See, Claire? This is me, *doing something* with my life. (Where does that leave your precious theories now, then?) Meeting people, breathing the wild freshness of the Northern Spanish air, smoking fine Moroccan weed, savouring the cheap rough red wine. Drinking life neat. Yeah, Claire. *Meeting new people*. People with stories. People who have *lived.* Dutch and Germans and English and Belgians. All sorts.

It's me and Joe out here. Friends = permanent. Lovers = temporary. (And no, Claire, if I may pre-empt your predictable question: we didn't pack our *beloved* Xbox.) Not that you'd care but Joe was chucked by Emma too. This, doubtless, will gladden the charred and smouldering remains of the thing that may once have beaten in your chest. (Memo from Joe re: you and him: The feeling was mutual.)

Later:

The blisters are a bitch, Claire, I'm not going to lie to you. But I will survive. You think I'll lay down and die, oh no, not I. You used to sing that, didn't you? You don't have a monopoly on get-up-and-go, Claire. I have gotten up and I've gone. I've been drinking Rioja all evening with Joe and a couple of Dutch blokes and an English girl named Kate. Oh, yes, she's pretty all right, Claire. Pretty, and the possessor of a fully functioning human heart. (Perhaps you could borrow it some time?) And she's walking with us tomorrow. Never fear; I'll keep you well posted.

Draft of letter continued, July 4th

I used to think, Claire, that there was some steaming pile of shite talked about the intensity of this whole Camino lark. But I've become a convert, on the rocky road to Santiago de Compostela. Oh, go ahead, laugh all you like. There's an opening up to beauty and to pain out here. I am opening up *to life.*

Ah, you just wouldn't get it.

The walking produces a kind of weariness that becomes – oh fuck it, I'm going to write it – transcendent. You walk hard, you play hard. Friendships are forged fast, in the white heat of life lived at full tilt. You fall in fast with people. I feel it now between Kate and myself. (Have I mentioned her prettiness, Claire? The chocolatey pools of her soft brown eyes, or the faint constellation of freckles spanning her button nose?)

So, we were stopped for lunch today. Joe had gone to locate a secluded spot in which to answer nature's call, so Kate and I were left alone for a while. As we chewed contentedly on our salami bocadillos, her hand suddenly brushed against my (only slightly sunburnt) knee.

'Wasp,' she said, and smiled.

'Oh, thanks,' I replied.

And then the second touch, a little more lingering, on the flimsiest of pretexts.

'Sorry, I left some breadcrumbs there.'

'There's no need to apologise,' I said, investing the words with rich meaning. Breadcrumbs indeed.

She smiled again, but coyly.

I do not think this touching was accidental. Did I mention that she's younger than you, Claire?

Draft of letter continued, July 5th

Kate, Joe and I continue. At one point along a narrow track, I walked directly behind our Yorkshire friend (for it's thence she hails). The sensuous twitching of her cheeks drove me near mad with desire. I walked for long stretches, Claire, with a mighty limp. (Clue: not blisters.) Life surges through me at high voltages these days!

Diary, July 5th

We encountered a trio of Bostonian meatheads at our albergue this evening. ('Dude,' one announced, 'a toast to the Irish!' Plastic Paddies – can't live with them, can't smother them in their sleep.) They eventually realised they were getting nowhere with Kate and went to seek their sport elsewhere. I then patiently waited for Joe to hit the sack, so that she and I might be alone. To be fair to him, he showed more stamina than usual.

'You thinking of turning in?' he asked around midnight.

'Nah, think I'll have another glass,' I replied. (I don't mind admitting that I was dead on my violently blistered feet.)

'Yeah,' he said, stifling a yawn. 'Me too. Will you have another, Kate?'

It was getting like chess, or Cold War missile tests. Your move, my move.

'Go on, then,' she said.

Joe, Joe, Joe. Poor deluded Joseph.

Joe. He hasn't seen the little looks Kate fires at me. None so blind etc.

Still. I'm sticking to the fucker like glue from now on.

Draft of letter continued, July 6th

Well, this little missive is proving longer than I'd planned. Events, as they say, have overtaken us. Life is *eventful*. I haven't so much as looked at an Xbox in over 80 hours. Eighty. Count 'em, Claire. Count 'em.

A few beers in a bar next to the albergue last night. With Joe standing there like Gooseberry-In-Chief, Kate eventually toddled off to bed. But make no mistake, tonight is the night. I feel its delicious slow pull. Kate and I draw closer daily. We talked about our families on the road today. She opened herself like some tender flower. Her parents divorced when she was twelve. As the eldest child, she was caught most in the crossfire. It was too long ago now to really matter anymore, she said. She seemed surprised to find her eyes damp at this moment. Stupid, stupid, she said. I chanced an arm round her shoulder. I met no resistance whatsoever. Her head lolling softly, sweetly against my chest.

I lightened the moment by telling her my parents were still together, though largely out of sheer spite. She laughed one of those blubbing laughs that emerge from crying people like points of light in the dark.

We talked of our exes. (I may have mentioned you in passing, Claire.) There were rueful nods, the sharing of wisdom hard won.

Honestly, Claire. I played a fucking stormer.

Diary, July 7th

Too exhausted for anything last night. Hit the hay early.

I returned to the albergue from a trip to an ATM this morning to find Joe and Kate huddled dangerously close and chuckling. Guffawing, even. Locked in a private universe of hilarity, they were.

'Will we make a start?' I said.

They collapsed in hysterics. She punched him in the arm. More playfully than I would have liked, if you want the truth. An emphatic belt of the knuckles would have been quite all right. It wasn't that sort of punch.

I managed to get next to her for part of the way. But during the inevitable stops and encounters with other walkers, I often lost my place. The air today smelt strongly of manure and eucalyptus. Mainly manure.

Diary, July 8th

That slight hiss you just heard? The sound of the gloves coming off.

Joe, over our breakfast of melon and espresso, tossing the words out like a careless fishing line.

'There's another route we could take today, through the hills. Spectacular views apparently. Although…' – the fucker actually paused, as though the thought had just struck him – '…maybe you'd want to go the easier route. On account of your blisters, like.'

'We,' he continued – this new we, according to the arithmetic taking shape, referring to Kate and himself, Lord and Lady Joe del Camino – 'could always go the long way and meet you beyond later? Up to you,' he added, spreading his upturned palms, as though this were a great indulgence on his part.

'Spectacular views?' I replied. 'I'm up for that. Blisters be damned!'

'Deadly,' he said. He managed the word, but the face? The face let him down something dreadful.

'I mean, you don't mind, do you?' I said.

'Jesus, no. Of course not. More the merrier.'

'Kate? You don't mind an invalid tagging along?' I said.

'No,' she said. 'Not at all.' These last three words came two heartbeats after the first. I counted the beats.

There was a fair whack of silence knocking around on the road today. There were dribbles of talk only, stalling fast to nothing.

<u>Draft of letter continued, July 8th</u>

I'm playing the long game with the lovely Kate. After all ~~care~~ Claire I feel quite sure this won't be some mere roll in ~~theee~~ the hay. No. There are deep connections between us. I feel our roots beginning to intertwine like ~~manifoew~~ magnificent redwoods. ~~And that no just the splifff talking. It's me, talking through the spliff. Her ass is incredible. Did I maybe say that before? Maybe did I.~~

Diary, July 9th

We went to a bar this evening.

'You look really nice tonight,' I said to Kate.

She sipped her drink.

'Thank you,' she said.

Then I waited for her to smile.

'How are your blisters now?' she said. 'They looked horrendous earlier.'

It was my turn to sip my drink. And by sip *I mean* copiously gulp.

Diary, July 10th

We arrived today in Sarria, my feet singing sharp with pain. My back joins in the chorus too these days, a creaky counterpoint. For the record, I am resting in the albergue and am wild hopped up on a cocktail of codeine, anti-inflammatories and vodka. (I took the precaution of packing a hipflask.) They're off, the other two, exploring. Exploring what, you might ask? The early Gothic church on Rua Maior? Or each other's tongues? I wouldn't be surprised.

<u>Later:</u>

Joe and Kate arrived back at the albergue five hours after they'd left. Five. (This is a small town.) They sat beside each other on Joe's bed. Closer, I would say, than was strictly necessary. They'd been drinking. I could see the flush of it in their faces.

'What time do you call this, then?' I mock-scolded, tapping my watch. I kept my tone judiciously light. The codeine and vodka were working their magic still. I had sent in reinforcements. I was performing a fine impression of a man far above the mere trivialities of the human heart.

'Must have lost track of the time, I suppose,' said Kate. Was that the hint of a smirk creeping round her lips?

'We stopped for a bite to eat too,' added Joe.

A <u>five-hour</u> bite to eat, I'm thinking.

'And a drink too,' I helpfully added.

'Yes,' said Kate, her brows lowering in perfect time with the mood. 'Is that all right?'

'Oh, of course. I'm hardly one to judge,' I said, taking a generous swig from the hipflask as an illustration of this.

The silence lay heavily a moment. Lower lips were chewed. Fingernails were examined. I broke the quiet. I gestured round the bare room.

'It's not the worst, this place, by the standards of where we've been staying.'

A heavier silence still fell. Kate glanced at Joe. Joe looked at the floor. Then he spoke.

'Eh, funny enough, I was actually thinking of checking into a hotel we passed earlier. It looked really nice. Treat myself.'

A deadly sap of viciousness rose in me.

'On your own, Joe? Will you not be lonely?'

The air in the room was all needles and pins.

'I was thinking of staying there too,' said Kate.

'Do you know, that sounds like a plan? Let's all treat ourselves,' I said.

'We've already checked in,' said Kate.

I emptied the hipflask in three seconds flat.

Diary, July 14th

I left them the other morning.

Joe had become too shit-eatingly smug for words. I could barely look at Kate. Granted, I was just a few moments ago looking at photographs of her on my phone. (Less pretty than once I thought. Far less, when you take a good long look at her. The eyes, really, the eyes are dead.)

The wine is cheap because it tastes fucking cheap. My stomach cries daily for mercy. I keep pouring it down there all the same.

Tomorrow, I walk. Again.

Diary, July 15th

Where are you tonight, Claire? Are you wandering the lonely halls of OKCupid *as once we each wandered them before the felicitous coincidence of our mutual liking of each other's pages? We were happy for a time, weren't we?*

The blisters are a fucking nightmare. My feet are a war zone, pocked, bloody, crumbling. My feet, my mind.

Postcard, sent July 16th

Dear Claire,

Was going to write a letter but thought I'd just keep it simple. I'll be home by the time you get this. Don't suppose you'd fancy a coffee some day?

T xx

HORSE FAIR · RACHAEL HEGARTY

My brothers are enchanted by ponies.
One after another, I name
as many as I can remember:

Connemara, Piebald, Kerry Bog,
Irish Draught, a white light racer
and the blackest black Irish Hunter.

The horses trot into Smithfield,
led by Travellers, reins and bit.
Heads high as the walking people's sky.

I pull my palm over the tongue and grove
of a yellow barrel wagon of ash wood.
Breath for the scent of windfall fires,

take in the small door, a raised bed,
and tell the little brothers
Mamo Mór might have lived in one, like this.

A man steps out from behind a horse and asks
Was she a Carroll? I nod my yes.
The Traveller smiles, you're every bar of a Carroll.

ON DOLLYMOUNT   KEVIN GRAHAM

The sense of two centuries,
a breeze lifting whimbrels and plovers
high into the air under crystal skies
that seem to go on forever. Along the banks

of hemlock and speedwell a breathless thing
like the inexorable tug of sorrow
following death. I'm here beside you, me being
your dad if only for the shadow

of a second. You won't remember
so let's just say we're cycling with your mum
towards the sea, that purple glitter
on up ahead. There's hours of the sun

left yet; the ice-cream man's going nowhere.
We'll examine stone after stone, wade
ankle-deep into frictionless water
and return to the shade

of the river they call time.
Memory is too narrow, too small. The truth is
the outline of our bodies floats plumb
against the earth and happiness buoys us.

ASK A TATTOOIST   D C CLIS

about true love –

all the Suzannes
smothered under Yin-Yangs

or Michaels devoured
by butterflies;

the Karens lasered off
with no more consideration

than bacon frying in a pan.
Or the Jasons

now stamped VOID,
as superfluous as a bounced cheque.

Ask a tattooist
about the fickleness of human nature,

the irresolution of erasure,
and the palimpsest of regret.

That the tendency of ink
is to waver enduringly

and the word made flesh
to deliquesce.

How everything reckoned
to a certainty

can so easily
be crossed out;

everything, that is,
except your birthmark.

About which he informs you,
regrettably –

nothing can be done.

FLUTTER   NIALL KEEGAN

It holds the older ones. The ones that still stand out however faded and scratched by the time they've spent. It holds the vague, yet familiar. The memories. The patterned caps. The talk. Most of all it holds the taps and the stools and the running horses. Those who come to sit and to watch and to lose. Over and over. Round and round. It sits on an east end street, tight between two buildings just as tall, just as old, and just as ubiquitous. One selling bets, the other selling cheap calls to anywhere in the world: call Bangladesh, call Trinidad, call India, Nigeria... I stop reading long before the poster has time to finish.

It faces out red and dirty. A neon sign flickers, grinding out a message against the sunlight. An eight-stringed harp limited in movement. The faint glow draws me in. The door is closed to the street and to anyone who might yet be undecided. Mirrored script is raised against a wooden backing. Juliet's. The letters reflect a series of slow, dull winks: the traffic they distort. Bending and stretching before finding shape.

The air is thick with dust. Fat enough to scribble on with a wet finger. It clouds the lungs and takes the throat. I stand and smoke. And itch and stiffen. After a final drag I stab my cigarette into a lamppost. I break its back against the scabby paint, and everything flakes to the ground. A temporary streak of ash stains the metal.

The streets are shrunk by stalls filled with vegetables I've never seen before, accompanied by mysterious shouts and veils that should seem totally out of place, but around here, are close to universal. It's all turnip bumps and hairy melons, neatly stacked, sheltered by tents streaky blue and white, borrowed from a beach scene. All the whiteness left in Whitechapel is crammed into the pubs and bookies. And I wonder if I fit in. My voice. My face. But quickly I realise that I don't care, and that I'm no longer smoking. I make my way toward it, careful to avoid the rabble.

I sidestep a mobility scooter parked near the entrance, noticing the jesus-fish bumper sticker preaching West Ham United and the British bulldog pissing on the single currency. I push through the door and instantly recognise myself if I ever reach sixty. The light and heat of the street is instantly suffocated, swallowed and held by bloated cheeks. The interior is a ballet of depression: each drinker's gaze rising up on a stiff toe, straining to notice, straining to be noticed. It smells the way grey might. The carpet is worn and shiny and randomly patterned with lines of duct tape, as if it has recently cut itself shaving. There's little dialogue, and no one talks louder than the eight or so televisions that ring the room, giving light to the ceiling and a dark pit to the floor. It's them that's in charge. The entire pub is sunk beneath, suffocated at the bottom of the well. The walls are stained with nicotine, streaked like a clamshell. Old men on the way out, spending their days milking every last drop of serotonin from their assorted addictions. All related through disease. All missing the same mother.

I order a pint by means of a raised eyebrow and shy wag of the finger. The barman is jerky, and looks like a dried-out mop, his Adam's apple cuts sharply from his throat whenever his lips or tongue move. He looks about as pleased as impotence can. I settle, knowingly resting my forearms in the sticky spills left on the counter, puddled beside red tops twisted to display the day's racing. It's all tiny horses and tiny jumpers. Scratchy blue circles waiting to be crunched up and collapsed. Waiting to be thrown away.

The barman docks a glass at the tap. White hair grows over his knuckles and black stains pleat around his fingernails. I stare down at my own hands. Reflectively. Achingly. Somewhat pretentiously. When I was younger, and just out of the bath, I'd stare at my fingertips all dried up, cursorily aged. My mother always warned me to get dry. Quick. Or you'll stay that wrinkly forever.

The glass descends to the counter filled with upward momentum. The settling sands I could watch forever. I grip it loosely, appreciating its weight. With time, the straightest line will cut the colours.

My eyes scan the altar behind the bar, filled with generic Irish clutter that could only be found in such a place, or perhaps, a barbers: Packie beating Romania, a Croke Park parade, some boxer standing over some other boxer in famous triumph. Amputated dreams long gone but still left throbbing. The phantom glory of home.

I left just as soon as I decided I had to go. Clumsy and hesitant. I soon recognised a feeling in myself that quickly became apparent in everybody else. I didn't want to talk about it, really. I didn't want anyone else to talk about it either. For some strange reason everyone who was leaving needed everyone else to know. They needed it heard, they needed it acknowledged: how much they hated the place, how much it screwed them over, how much they'd never come back. What a flying crying fucking shame it was. I didn't care about that. I just wanted my life to feel like it was finally getting started, having stalled at the first set of traffic lights. Sounded out by whoever it was who sat behind me leaning on their horn.

The Irish voices inside the pub don't shudder and repel me like the ones I hear on the tube or at work or at some random house party where your cock is still measured in cans. Phrases and sounds I'm accustomed to but have never heard like this. Sounds I always ignored or sneered at back home. Certain words are still stroked the same: The men. Your man. Your one. I turn and look at the faces, which are just as cracked and distorted as the voices they carry. Randomly thrown together as cobblestones. Hard life can be seen. Holes drank and smoked through stomachs. A pepcid for every pint. Scepters of rolled-up newspaper. The screams of faster, finish, fuck. And then, without warning, the wet slap of a mop:

'So what has ya in so? The racing?'

'Me. No. Nothing. Just hiding from the weather I suppose.'

'Ay. Ay. Tis a lovely day out der alright.'

We spend a few awkward seconds in silence. Man to mop. But he leaves when he's called… and he's off… to the other end of the bar. My eyes follow him halfway but are blocked by a gentleman slumped, motionless, sitting in front of what must be the queue for the dishwasher. Glasses of all values are scattered at his elbows, dregs of foam and ice and beige and amber. I stare and I wonder. Can they all be his? This drinker. Like seeing a dog up a tree, first you'd be astonished, then you'd be impressed, before ultimately being gravely concerned for the dog's wellbeing. I continue to glance, but he never moves. Except for his feet, they keep tapping on the bottom rung of the stool. The same steady pace. Like a dreaming dog.

The men's existent is one of small victories over small distances. Waiting for the pub to finally open. Waiting for their wives to finally stop. Waiting for their piss to finally break. No crying. No comparing of hardships. In many ways I'm jealous of the simplicity. To have so little to pursue. How I'm too young to give up. How there's still too much hope. How there's still things left to throw away. How that couldn't be accepted.

*

Oliver Twist drifts around the bar collecting money and directions from those too feeble-minded, feeble-bodied, or inebriated to take the sixteen or so steps to the bookies next door. I can tell from across the room there's crisps in his hair and he's been washing his face with lemonade. By the time he clears the tables and has worked his way over to the high chairs the man slumped to my right explodes like a pile of kicked leaves. He straightens and frantically burrows through his pockets, finally emerging with a crumpled betting slip for the young mogul to cash. He welcomes him over by placing his hand far too low on his back and offering him the stale yellow dregs of a Guinness. I try not to look directly at them. It's all nods and grunts and shadows. The boy hums. His eyes, level with the bar, never leave the wood.

I know nothing about horseracing, and less about placing bets. There's a list of horses on the screen above but it might as well be the third round from Augusta or the results of the Eurovision.

The anticipation swells as the next race approaches. The men all line up in front of the screens as their monkeys mount their shoulders. From what I understand from the hushed whispers and increased level of bullshitting – this is the big one. There's talk of 'soft ground' and 'travels well'. I even hear: 'he comes out like the dregs of the toothpaste'. Everyone talks like they know the jockeys personally or own a stake themselves. Like they understand. Like they're owed this one. In reality all they have is the monkeys on their backs telling them to drink, to gamble, to fight. To sooth their suspicions. Touched by their memories more than their senses. And then touched by a hand on my shoulder:

'Son ... Son.'

'Hum ... Yeah. What?'

'Hoi Polloi in the third. If you're interested. You look like you're interested, son.'

'_____'

'The third race, son. If you're looking. It's worth a flutter. Easy money now.'

'Yeah, cheers, thanks. I might do.'

'No bother. Just go tell the youngfella.'

The man is gone just as some questions arrive. Replaced by the youngfella. The youngfella already knows. He knows the race. He knows the horse. And he offers his thoughts on what's a reasonable sized bet.

'_____'

'Run you worthless fuckin' donkey. You fuckin' monkey. Ruuun.'

Once involved, my humanity soon slips. I join the line of shadows. Everything is fixed against the constant beat of the race. The noise of the hooves and the steady hum of the commentator rattling like a sowing machine. I can't tell where my horse is coming. I shout to avoid suspicion. My eyes can't hold the screen, the pulp of colour and the galloping stems. So instead I focus on the man who gave me the tip, surely he'd back his own advice. Surely he has a tell, a sign, a twitch to show me we're right. To show me we're winning. I study his leanings. His movements. He reaches higher up on his toes, hoping to somehow influence the race, to stretch out our horse, to whip the animal himself. His head juts sharply towards the screens, barely seen amidst the tangle of sleeves and hats and heads. The closer the race comes to finishing, the more punters leave the action, heads bowed, tickets torn and thrown. The race is run. There is a general sense of relief, a communal exhale, followed by gripes and sparkling observations from the crowd: '… sure, he was never running fast enough.'

The men return to their various stations around the pub. To their burnt broken glass. More and more leave until eventually only one man is left. The pearl. He removes a fob watch from his top pocket, opens it, but never checks the time. He knows the time. It's returned after a short pause, a short pose, a short parade. Hard to figure the design, whether filigree or scrapes. He stares. He nods. And his eyes sparkle in a wave. His plated tooth, whether gold or bronze or tin, holds the faintest light. A real discoball, this fucker. This gambler.

Beaten, I order a pint and a whiskey, forgetting which one is the chaser. The chat melts away. All that's left is the screech sparkling from the gambler's fob. Standing in the corner, back to the wall, checking the length of his sleeves. I want to ask. And I want to argue. To swing my bones around the bar looking for anything to cut. But instead I just sip reverently at my whiskey, pretending to notice the oak, the smoke, the leather. Waiting for it. Reaching for it. It never comes, but I trust that it's there. These drinkers. These gamblers. And underneath I'm glad to lose. I want them to know I could be anywhere else but I chose to be here.

I pick up a tiny blue bookie pen and carve my name into the counter. My first time round.

A GHAZAL FOR DARTMOOR   CHLOE FIRETTO-TOOMEY

Mum and I drive out of the city to Dartmoor –
wild ponies move like the shadows of starlings across the moor.

Sundew and cranberry sweep raw slopes of minerals and peat,
and we recognise the height of the spearmint-blasted moor.

First light falls on the stone circle pink as spun sugar. Across the bog
is heathland and tors – stacked granite hilltops blot the moor.

We are at the edge of the world where the gorse grips the precipice.
We are eyelevel in the face of immensity, ocean thrashing the shards of
the moor.

It seems silence was invented here by the wind's cleavage.
We follow stone rows to a ruined farmhouse on the abandoned moor,

and find a pathway to monoliths, run our hands over ancient stones
and medieval tombstones that whisper to the open moor.

Cows trim the edge of a cliff; we look up to take pictures.
Grasses graze the sky like brush strokes kissing the moor.

Chloe: from the Greek meaning *flourishing green shoot.* I steal a stream-
stone,
hold hands with it to remember us walking the moor.

ORANGES   FRANK FARRELLY

(circa 1974)

My parents sent me oranges and home-made bread.
Others received Weetabix, Rice Krispies, jars of Nescafé.
It made me stand out, a kind of charity case,
though friends said nothing to offend
– they loved the bread, especially with marmalade.

I'd hide the oranges inside my locker, out of view,
for it was cool to stink of cigarettes or chewing gum
but oranges, oranges were in the league of buttoned cuffs
and polished shoes and homework always done.

Sunday afternoons that made you feel the world was dead
and you were left behind, I'd take one to the lake and sit
beneath the willow tree and cut it with my army knife
and peel it cleanly from the skin and eat it like a secret swallowed whole,
then wash the odour from my hands – though bouquets lingered on.

for I remember Haydar from the Lebanon who never had a visitor
and whiled his Sundays on the tennis court practising his serve,
and once, going to the refectory, stopped me on the steps
and said how much he loved the way I smelled, then smiled,
closed his eyes and slowly opened them again,
as if he had been asked to picture somewhere beautiful.

A SHIP CAME FROM VALPARAISO   DONAL HAYES

Before my life began, I lived at the start of the Straight Road, a road that stretched for about three miles along the banks of the River Lee from the edge of Cork city toward Kerry. There were yellow street lights out as far as the Maxol filling station and after that, darkness. On the far side of the road was a footpath that just stopped after the filling station, there was no destination, it existed for a while and then stopped.

I went to primary school on Mardyke Walk and to secondary school across the road from that. University was between home and the primary school, so by the time I had graduated from university with a BA in Irish and Geography, I had lived my entire life within about two square miles.

Joanne was my girlfriend then (in latter times) and she and I would have sex in the field up past the garage and sometimes in her bed if her parents were away. It was woolly, awkward, brambly sex, hard negotiated through jumpers and duffel coats. Sometimes it ended in climax and sometimes not. We knew no better.

For my 21st birthday Joanne bought me a ticket to go on holiday with her to Madrid. It would be my first trip out of Ireland and with open return tickets our freedom had no bounds.

Except, the night before we left, she split up with me. She couldn't face a moment more and in a theatrical sweep she tore up her flight ticket. I was careful to keep mine intact.

She had been drinking gin and it had taken the legs of a truth serum. It was like she couldn't stop herself once she had started I now know the top fifty reasons why she thinks I'm hideous. That was enough for me to be getting on with.

That's all just background though. That's how I happened to be here, all alone in the late afternoon of tar-sticky heat of summer in Madrid. Ripe fruit, ripe flowers, hanging in the dead air.

I was outside a small hotel in La Latina and there was a huge copper relief sculpture of a horse and a bull fighting over a broken sword, the searing sun behind it making it shimmer. What was it saying? Sometimes the bull wins? Sometimes the matador has to die.

The taxis were still on siesta so walking towards culture was the only option.

Luckily there was a bar open beside me and it looked cool. I sat by the counter and ordered a cold San Miguel.

'Buenas tardes,' a voice said beside me. 'Puedo tener una cigarillo por favor.'

'Yo no habla Espanol,' I stumbled, turning to the most beautiful face I had ever seen.

'I was asking you for a cigarette.' She smiled in a friendly way I would not have been used to.

'Help yourself.' I passed the packet of Major and the Zippo along the bar to her.

'Extra size,' she read suggestively. 'They don't look particularly big to me.'

'They have it in the girth,' I heard myself say. Joanne was right – I was nothing short of hideous. They have it in the girth. Lordy Lordy.

'You American?' the goddess asked, putting the cigarette between two soft pink lips where it hung like she was Lauren Bacall in *The Big Sleep*.

'No,' I said. 'Irish.'

'Viva Bobby Sands.' She smiled and raised her fist in a revolutionary salute.

'Viva Bobby Sands,' I agreed, raising my fist awkwardly.

She was speaking again but I was not listening.

Her lips were moist and pink and shiny and her tongue darted to the top of her teeth as she spoke.

'Say that again,' I said.

'What – cerveza?'

'Yes,' I said, almost hoarsely. No other word in any language required more tongue flicking.

'Cerveza, I was just asking for a beer,' she laughed.

The longer the conversation went on, the more nervous I became. There was real evidence that I was being chatted up by the most beautiful girl in the world.

'Patrick,' I said, putting my hand out to shake hers – she held on a moment too long and we both knew it. She may as well have said 'come to bed.'

'So, Patrick, what are you doing in my city?'

'I'm,' – long pause for lying, – 'working.'

'And what do you work at, Patrick?' asked the Goddess.

'I am a poet. I write poetry.'

And where in the name of God did that come from? A poet no less. I was in a new place now and I could be whatever I wanted to be. I was only surprised I managed to keep my own name. I could have ended up as Fingal or Raph or even Marco. Beer and tequila and the liberation of being a person with no history were taking over. I was starting to feel free for the first time in a long time – maybe for the first time ever.

'Would you like to smoke, Patrick?' she said – saying Patrick in a way that clearly indicated that the word meant Love God in Spanish.

'Why not?'

We sat outside beneath an orange tree and lit a long joint of grass and tobacco mixed.

'Now this is extra size.' She smiled as she lit the twisted end of the Rizla.

She held the joint elegantly and the grass crackled as she took in waves of the sweet subversive smoke. After a few hits she passed the joint to me. Her lips had just touched this and now mine were too. We were practically married, for God's sake.

She leaned over, resting her head on my shoulder, her long black hair warm in the afternoon sun.

'Will you write about me, Patrick?'

Would I hell.

Tháinig long ó Valparaiso,
Scaoileadh téad a seol sa chuan,
Chuir a hainm dom i gcuimhne
Ríocht na Gréine, Tír na mBua.

I whispered to her as she lay beside me in the orange garden. I was Pablo Neruda, I was Robert Browning, I was John Keats. I was every romantic poet who ever lived, with a stolen verse from Pádraig de Brún.

A ship came from Valparaiso,
Dropped its anchor in the harbour,
Her name reminded me of countries,
Sunlit countries far away.

A childhood poem, a joint of grass and a glass of tequila and before anyone could yell plageristico bastardo she was in my arms. The matador never had a chance.

In the morning we sat in her kitchen and drank fresh orange juice and strong black coffee. The sun was bright, the birds sang and my new life stretched before me across the red-tiled rooftops of Salamanca.

Today she would show me Madrid.

'You have arrived, Patrick, for the fiesta of San Isidro, the patron saint of Madrid, she has brought you as a gift to the people of Madrid. You will write great things about my city. And we will be in love.'

And we were in love. In love to the backdrop of the Guernica. To the twisted, tormented, passion of Madrid. From the Prado to the museos to the backstreet bars of Salamanca. Nothing was as it seemed, alone or collectively, it was different each time you looked. The agony of the burnt-out twisted past, a mother holding her dead child, a screaming horse, a dove with a broken wing. And, skateboarding by the heavy symbols of their recent history, tanned boys in white t-shirts leapt in a timeless dance before pretty young girls.

We drank and smoked and ate olives and garlic soup. We laughed and kissed and sat in silence. The sex of my youth, fumbling through layers of damp wool to get to reluctant cold flesh, was replaced by the aching demands of this naked tanned beauty.

'Tell me some more beautiful words,' my Goddess whispered.

'Gluais, ar sí, ar thuras fada,

Liom ó scamall is ó cheo,

Tá fé shleasaibh gorm Andes

Cathair scáfar, glé mar sheod.'

I touched the rhythm on the drum of her stomach.

'Come along with me,' she whispered.

Far from cloud and mist, for you'll

Find beneath the Andes Mountains,

An awesome city, bright as a jewel.'

I gently kissed the Andes Mountains and slowly headed to the awesome city.

Later, we sat beneath the fountain at the Plaza Jesus and the mist cooled us like the Andean dawn.

'I need to tell you something, Patrick.'

There was a long silence.

'Is it something from the past?' I asked. 'Something that has already happened?'

'Yes. Something…'

'Stop. Then I don't want to know.'

Again silence.

'Tell me something of the future,' I said.

I tapped out more poetry and the rhythm of the day began to build.

Around the corner onto the Plaza Jesus came a marching band led by men dressed entirely in white with red neckerchiefs beating huge drums.

Behind them came the brass section and then a statue of San Isidro held shoulder high. A large crowd followed them dressed in the traditional costumes of the penitent, long robes and the pointed masked hats of mourning.

It struck me that this would be what the end of the world would be like.

Darkness fell and fireworks began exploding high above the plaza. We fell into another bar and started drinking vodka and Coke. The bar was heaving with people, many holding silver crucifixes or with crosses embroidered onto beautiful old silk vestments. Something on the television caught my eye.

America seemed to be on fire. The Goddess translated. The cops in the Rodney King case had been found not guilty and Los Angeles had exploded. Riots and fires tore through the City of Angels and swept across the United States. The National Guard was holding the country together.

Someone heard I was Irish and came over to tell me there was an Irish band playing in the plaza tonight. A very famous Irish band.

I touched a large silver cross around his neck and as I did the television changed from the Rodney King story to a picture of Bishop Eamon Casey of Galway. A picture of a solemn and yet jovial-looking Casey sat beside the newsreader.

'What's happening?' I asked the Goddess.

'There is a bishop in Ireland who has fathered a child and has absconded from the parish with the church funds.'

'You are shitting me.' I stared at the photo of the well-known bishop.

'No, honestly.'

There will surely be no dawn.

This is it.

Almost on cue the band outside in the plaza threw out a few power chords to test the volume of their equipment. Feedback from a speaker sounded like screaming across the square.

'Ladies and Gentlemen – An Emotional Fish.'

The rhythm of the drums started almost to the beat of marching band, joined by the hammer blows of the electric guitar.

See that's the trouble with reality, it's taken far too seriously

I do hope God is good to me and Santa Claus to the children

The singer snarled the words into his microphone.

I took the Goddess's hand and ran to the centre of the plaza.

'This is it', I shouted to the Goddess. 'This is it.'

I tore off my shirt and danced in the searing heat.

Celebrate

This party's over

I'm going home

Celebrate

This party's over

I'm going home

I try to think straight but the drink and the grass and the screaming music combine to make any kind of thinking difficult but the one clear thing is I am not going home. Pictures flash before me like my own personal Guernica, a pastiche of my past, a record of my battle, creation emerging from destruction. There is Joanne, the Straight Road, Doc Martens, my mother smiling, holding hands with Bishop Casey. Matadors, fires and doves and little bowls of olives, and my Goddess with her perfect teeth, pink lips and warm brown skin. And a ship from Valparaiso with a cross shaped mast so bright it shines like gold sailing up the River Lee in Cork, bringing its precious cargo to the heart of the city.

DETOUR (LEAVING EDINBURGH)   ROSAMUND TAYLOR

It took some time to admit we were lost.
That a train could be lost. I always held
my breath high in my chest until we crossed
the Forth Bridge, when the firth swelled
grey under us – the stretch, the too-wide
stretch of waves and rock, the wet clouds
bisected by red struts – and then I sighed,
a rough gasp, every time, even in crowds,
even on a 6am commute. But that day we never
crossed, never edged cold beaches in Fife
and, much later, the voice small and slivered,
the announcement came: we were in Stirling. Life
unsettled, we simmered on polyester seats.
    Then I saw the river. River and willow tree, grey
    shape of an old rowing boat, the beat
    of oars. The water was slow-moving that Sunday
    in September, the light thin. I was nineteen;
    I was in love. And I let go: I'd been
    holding that breath until I saw the river,
    the willow leaves falling onto the river.

THROW ME DOWN SOMETHING   ANN EGAN

Ladies of fairy dresses, floating feathers.
Lords of frock coats and high hats.
Shower me with your coins aplenty.
For I am dancing with the waters.

My bare toes grip sliding stones.
I'm in my spot under Feale's Bridge.
My brothers own the other arches.
The seventh one is mine, all mine.

Throw me down something.
Throw me down something.

The Feale flows full of sparkling trout.
I tip my fingers out for your coppers.
Porter for my father, a shawl for my mother.
You cross over to the Listowel Races.

Cross your palms, I'll sing your luck.
My hands turning like salmon leaping.
Silver scales and falling crowns.
I will tell you your fortune.

Throw me down something.
Throw me down something.

Three fine Feale geese are sleeping.
Me, I'm battling racing currents.
Blue ribbons and tails swishing.
Your horse will win the golden crock.

I'm clinging to pebbles and pennies.
Cheers and cries of all the people.
We'll move on, change our ditches.
Fine Lords and Ladies of Listowel Races.

Throw me down something.
Throw me down something.

SUDDENLY   GERALD DAWE

Fog everywhere – fog in the trees,
in the chimney pots, in the hedges,
at the street corner, in the railings,

fog on the roofs of the offices and
fog in the garden; fog horns sounding
on the bay that is invisible, fog horns

in the house like a ground-swell,
the sound of childhood in the dark
of early morning, fog in your eyes,

in your hair, fog horns that come
from somewhere deep down,
the unnerving fog, the blood-pulse.

JULY CLOUDS   SHARON FRAME GAY

"July clouds don't come up, they rain out where they are." Truer words were never spoken by my great grandmother. Down here in the low country of the Carolinas, summer days are hot as Hades, and at night it feels like the Devil himself is walking you home.

My name is Phadre. I live here on this parched plantation with my momma and two sisters, Hussy and Bo. I was born and raised in the weathered one-room cabin that we share. My momma and sisters work up at the house, cooking and cleaning. I was born with a milky eye. It looks like an egg that hadn't quite cooked yet. Folks say they don't want to look at my face when they're eating dinner, so I'm a field hand, and been wrestling with the tobacco since I can remember.

Day after day, it's the same. The rows of tobacco wave dark and dusty in neat lines that stretch clear up to the sun. We stoop and pick, then straighten, move on to the next leaves, do it all again. We watch for snakes hiding under the leaves. Most times, they're harmless, but every once in a while there's a Copperhead, and if you get bit, you might be thrashing in your bed for days praying for the doctor. It depends on how valuable you are, if they'll be sending him. Me, I don't think I'd ever set eyes on that doctor, so I work carefully, parting the leaves with trepidation, my fingers moist with fear even though the rest of me is dry as kindling.

Every day, we are drenched in sweat before the sun has barely risen. The sky is white as though the blue were boiled out by the heat, bleached and sullen. I don't wear shoes. I keep my one pair for winter, so my feet are calloused and hard as a goat, but still I feel the red clay beneath them like Satan is holding a match to my soles. I want to sink down under a tree and rest a while when the sun is straight overhead. Even the crows are walking, following us down the rows, their mouths open with thirst, hoping to peck at some sweat or spit as we work.

I looked down the row and saw the overseer, Hutchins, coming this way on his big black Tennessee Walker named General. General's so mean, he'd think nothing of knocking you down with his massive shoulder, then stepping right on you, or biting your arm like he was eating a cob. You'd be lucky he doesn't break your bones. Worse yet is the bullwhip Hutchins has coiled around the saddle horn, just waiting to unfurl and take a piece of your skin home for supper. When we see General, we work faster and keep our heads down.

I am 17 years old. An age to marry, or be sold. There's a war starting up. There's a lot of rattling of sabres and big talk down in town that we're gonna start whupping some Yankees. Folks are getting restless, worrying about their crops and their stock and wondering about the future. I don't know what they're going to do with me. Marry me off or sell me, maybe either way I'll end up somewhere else, away from my family. It worries me nights, and nobody says nothing that can quiet me. They're all worried too. I don't think I stand a chance to get a husband or do anything more than work in the fields until I die. Some days, it just feels hopeless.

I stopped to wipe my face, and big Joss came up quietly on the other side of the row. He whispered, 'There's a man some nights comes down to the river. He's looking to see if anybody wants to ride the train.' I froze for a second, then nodded my head quickly, as Joss moved on by. Even talking about the Underground Railroad can get you beat, or worse. I ain't seen many who run away ever come back. You never know what happens to them. Those that the big dogs find are sold off, beaten, or hanged. It gives me the shivers just thinking about it, even in all this heat. How could I leave my momma and sisters. How could I find my way across all those miles to freedom. My mind kept rubbing up against it, until it's chaffed and sore from thinking, and I want to cry just with the agony of it all. Then I saw General bearing down on me, and I practically ran down the row, my guilt and fear keeping time with his steady trot.

That night, after the sun gave up, I took myself down to the river. I didn't know what to do, so I sat on a big rock and stared into the darkness. All I heard around me were night sounds, crickets, owls, but mostly silence. Finally, I came back to the cabin and tried to sleep, but I was still awake when shafts of dawn streamed in through the cracks in our walls. I trekked down to that old river six times, until one night I hear a low voice in the thicket. 'Girl, you want to ride the train?' My breath hitched in my chest, and I nodded. A short nod, like maybe not a nod at all. I braced for the sting of that old bullwhip of Hutchins and hoped he wouldn't get my other eye. But instead the voice said, 'Come back in two days' time – that's when the moon is out of the sky. Don't bring nothing with you. Rub your arms and legs with cow or pig shit so the dogs can't smell you so good, and don't tell nobody.' A rustle in the bushes, and he was gone.

The next two days were hard to bear. We picked leaves and climbed those rows up to the sun and back. My hands were bleeding and my back ached. I prayed for rain, even though it could ruin the crops. 'Just rain on me, God', I prayed, 'and let me cool off.' But the summer sky slapped the top of my head and the stones in the row rolled under my feet, just to make me fuss.

The next day, the overseer trotted up to me on General. 'Phadre, run on up to the garden and pick some onions for your momma, and bring them to the kitchen for her, ya hear?' I nodded and straightened up, grateful to leave the field, stretch my legs. In the garden, I sampled a bite of lettuce, and pulled several green onions out of the ground, dusted them off on my skirt. They looked white and milky, just like my eye – staring back at me with accusations. I hid them behind my back and walked to the back door of the huge house and knocked. Momma answered. 'Phadre. What you doin' here?' I showed her the onions, and she took them in her hand like a bouquet of bitterness, then looked around and said, 'You best get back now – Hutchins be waiting for ya.' I looked into her eyes and said, 'I love you, Momma.' She smiled. 'I love you, too, baby, but get along now and I'll be seeing you tonight.' I turned and whispered, 'Goodbye Momma', and a murder of crows followed behind me, drinking my tears as they hit the path back to the field.

That night, I lay in bed with my arms crossed over my chest, like a dead person, my eyes wide open. I heard my sisters and momma breathing deeply. I was wishing I was them. When the dark was full and the entire plantation was cloaked in silence, I slipped from my bed and took my shoes, curled out the door like smoke, my shadow hugging the buildings down to the barn, towards the river. I rubbed cow shit all over my arms and legs and set out on the moonless trail.

'Where you going, Phadre?' a voice whispered in the darkness. I stopped still, then slowly stepped off the path into the bushes. Hiding behind a Loblolly Pine was my sister Hussy. She had followed me. 'You go on back to the cabin, Hussy,' I said, turning towards her, my hands clenched. We touched fingers in the shadows. I reached up, finding a tear on her cheek. I wiped it with my thumb and put it to my lips. I'm already gone. I'm a ghost now. How does she even see me, I thought. My heart was pounding in my chest. All I could think of was General and that bullwhip and those big dogs.

I turned and started to melt into the pitch, grazing the bushes with my skirt, leaving my scent for those dogs. Reaching down, I pulled off my skirt, handed it to Hussy, feeling vulnerable in ragged drawers, but there was nothing I could do. 'Take these back home with you,' I said softly. Hussy whispered again, 'Where you goin, Phadre?'

I turned back one more time. 'Don't you tell nobody you saw me, Hussy. Don't you tell nobody. I'm going North where the clouds rain out.' Somewhere in the darkness, there was the single cry of an owl, calling me to the river. The lonesome breeze smelled like freedom.

SHE WALKS   BERNIE CRAWFORD

She walks because the men with guns could rape her
She walks because her mother told her to

She walks because the men with bombs will kill her
She walks to keep up with the others

She walks because the dark shadows under her bed
now live in every room of her home

She walks because her school is a heap of stones
with pieces of porcelain ink wells sparkling among them

She walks because the stall where she bought
falafels in pitta pockets is gone

She walks because the tattered sneakers of the boy,
who sold spices in newspaper cones, lie among the rubble of the market

She walks because it is easier to walk than to stop
She walks because she is a child

She walks to find the piece that flew from her heart,
out through her mouth, the day the air strikes started

She walks to forget the piece that flew from her heart
that day the air strikes started

She walks

BIRDBOY   JOHN DAVIES

When he was first held out to me:
a trembling parcel of awkward bones,
translucent skin, inkscrawl of veins;
skein of flesh knitted both arms to his ribs.
The balls of his eyes skittered beneath glistening lids,
gummed hair in clumps the colour of hay.
Spindles of legs no use to him, his fused feet
grasping the bedsheets like fists.

Years until he learnt to translate the urge,
to restrain the soaring blood; change the course of air.
The sky quickened its vapours –
on cue, the clouds cleared a path;
he flew. Over the meadow his burgeoning form
thrown back by the early brook;
grey shadow cloaking the cows, awestruck as penitents.
It was the day my boy was seven.

A shrill you can hear half a mile away,
when his rolled tongue flits across ungiving palate
and he whistles; struggling to trace the shapes of words.
Across the rumble and dip of green fields, corn fields,
hidden fields of crows; nothing has moved for centuries
but my boy, his shadow dripping from a stoved-in abbey,
window-places gaping like unearthed skulls –
the *reilig* he roars through.

But the fear looms each morning
that he will keep on for the eye-line,
soar against the burning haze of the horizon,
brimming red as his first-opened eyes;
rise against the gathering clouds like ash flung from fire,
all aspect of his soul in ascension, sun-flared;
his shrill and keen growing fainter
until only heard in dream.

NUMBER SIX   PATRICK CHAPMAN

I miss the lock when I try the key but after a scraping attempt I find it and the door creaks too loud and I don't wait to shut it but stumble through into the kitchen and run to the sink full of dirty dishes. I bend over and throw up in it. There, it's done. I know what I've done. I'll wash the whole mess up before I go to bed, or maybe in the morning before you wake up.

I know what I've done. Too much wine on top of too much beer. I have talked all night about nothing. I have offended some, by my presence alone. No one mentioned you at all. They must have intended to be kind by keeping it light but they were not kind and they did not keep it light. I tuned out anyway so that as the evening dragged I hardly heard what any of them said. By the end of it all I was merely a rock in their stream of conversation.

I finish retching. Slowly I straighten up. Then I grimace at my reflection in the kitchen window, willing that pale copy of me to take it all, to take everything, to walk away into the grey with it, and vanish. I could live without my reflection, that future ghost constructing itself out of my diminishing remains yet a part of me wishes for oblivion, a pale suicide by light. It is already happening. My reflection is looking well these days. My reflection is looking better than me.

Once I was not the kind to seek company. Before you came, I would stay in all week, reluctant to meet the world. I was wrapped up in books, a shelf full of vinyl; and an obsession with *The Prisoner* to the extent that for my holidays I took the pilgrimage to Portmeirion every year. Solitary I was, and planning to stay that way, for we are each our own Number 1.

That was years ago, before you singled me out one night at a *Prisoner* SIG meeting. You insisted I come with you to another pub. You had something you wanted to discuss with me about George Markstein. It turned out that you didn't. You knew his name but had only a passing interest in the show. You'd had your eye on me for weeks. You used to see me at the meetings and liked it when I said the less said about the American remake, the better. That showed integrity, apparently. You decided that you wanted to get into my pants, and prayed that they didn't have Leo McKern's face on the back. That night in the other pub, we went on what became a date. Over the following two years we danced, kissed awkwardly, held hands, swore love. You had plans for us. It was wonderful and real and inexplicable to me. When we got married it was on a beach with a Zorb ball as our backdrop so we could pretend that Rover was the best man.

Our life now is a kind of remake, every day the same episodes but not done as well. I have lately needed to go out into the world. I have needed to not be here. You have encouraged me, told me to go, to leave you at home for God's sake, that you will be ready for company later, that you need to be alone. I must leave you alone.

I turn my back on the spectral reflection and remember something you told me early on. You said that as teenagers, you and your girlfriends would pass around tales of how you'd first been handled by some pre-pubescent wunderkind who thought himself majestic, suave despite his acne. Finding a demand for your favours, even from a pathetic specimen, you took account of the currency of love. I asked if this was universal, this sharing of evidence, or if it was just what you and your friends would do, like sea dogs showing off their shark bites. You did not know the answer, but the first experience for each of you was a benchmark, soon surpassed. You and your friends would complain of gropes and kisses, and compare notes. Was it down your blouse from behind, or up the back from in front? The slipping of a brassiere strap, the loosening of calico, the liberating of a button – all marked out of five, for no one was ever a six or more than a three. You would nearly always stop the game, with finger-handcuffs on the wrist or a tongue inside his ear. As you grew older, you became ever more disappointed by the clumsiness of boys, and came to understand the value of what they themselves had to offer. It was the law of supply and demand, which you found worked to your benefit. You kept them wanting but never getting much; there was no point in giving away the shop. What was the utility of love if you did not put a price on it? This was the wisdom your mother handed down to you, and her reasoning seemed sound to you then. Love was never free. Ours was to involve a transaction too. If I was good, if I waited, if I wanted you enough, I could have what you told me I wanted. I accepted your terms. I did not approach you sexually. I waited two years until you decided that it was time. We slept together that night at your place. It was nothing special for either of us.

When we married, you promised me that ours was not unconditional love, as your mother believed it impossible. Fourteen months after our wedding we found out that your mother was wrong. Unconditional love exists. It exists and we feel it, and it is physical. Unconditional love carries within it risk of unbearable pain.

Now I hear the springs of your bed as you stir. You are sleeping in the boxroom again tonight. You did not want to put me out, but each night I feel the expanse of our conjugal bed as an absence pulling me into its depths. You are wrapped in the sleeping bag pulled tight against the chance that I might try to enter. I will not, for we are past that now.

I wipe my mouth with the dishcloth and throw it in the sink and hope that you did not hear me, that I did not disturb you. I stagger back and taste the sharpness of the scorched trail the vomit has left in my throat. In the fridge I find a half-gone bottle of red beside the milk. It's not natural to keep red wine in the fridge but I don't care. I grab the bottle and thumb the cork all the way in and let the fridge door shut itself. The wine tastes like mould has proliferated inside it and I lose my bearings as my head swims towards a red horizon rising and falling against a green sky. The cork makes a compass of the bottle. I sit at the table and swig again, and it is awful, this two-day-opened Merlot.

I remember a day last winter when I captured a spider and pinned it to the kitchen door with a yellow tack. It made you think of an AWACS plane crossed with a Mars lander. Then you called me an astronaut. You said I don't belong on this planet. Of course you were right. I nodded, imagining myself in the dark, my tether fraying even in a frictionless environment. You pull it in, drawing me to safety but I cut the cable free at my end and wheel away into nothing.

The cold whistles in through the open front door and down the corridor to wrap me in chilled air. What am I doing, shivering here while you sleep alone upstairs? It isn't fair on either of us. I know that even in your dreams, you mourn our little angel but do you not believe that I mourn her too? 'We can always have another,' you said this morning as I left for work. You were trying to be kind but you were not. We will never have another. There will never be another one of her, our nameless child who lies beneath a small black marker in the angels' field. Without her I may as well be stranded on that cork adrift inside the bottle. As I put it down I catch the impossible reflection of faces captured in the green glass, the two of us together as never before.

PREPARING THE WAIT   ARTHUR GOODHILL

'I will build a bookcase,' I said
Made as I want it, instead
the compromise of ready made
cut and measured by youthful trade
kiln dried, cut wood and finest tread
But I need the wood first!

'I will fell the finest tree!' I said
white deal risen high this dawn
will fall to aid the plans I've drawn
and the awe of my craft will surely spread
but what is wood without the means to shape it?

'I will buy the finest tools!' I said
And settle for naught that won't astound
The thinnest blade and the sharpest edge
With tungsten tip and diamond pledge
But what of these blades all shaped so keen?
A thought to keeping safe the scene!

'I will buy the gilded cloth!' I said
No expense to spare for my fragile head
Nor fear for fingers or maiming limbs
With cloth to swerve all swaying trims

'I will build a bookcase!' I said
Then with tools and timber, retired to bed
Kept warm by the gilded cloth I wore
And slept easy, books strewn across the floor.

FUR COAT AND NO KNICKERS   LOUISE G COLE

Drawing breath between tales of dead
little brothers and elderly neighbours
moved away, my mother looks inside
a lifetime that's 92 and counting,
claims no-one's visited for months,
thinks I'm her cousin Betty
with designs on her fur coat and hopes
of borrowing a fiver.
I try not to mind the care home smell
and wonder what else to talk about when
the devil himself taps my shoulder
suggests I unburden, reveal secrets
never before shared, so I offer a revelation:
I lost my virginity four times
before I was married. She's never yet listened to me
so it's no surprise she doesn't hear,
continues with a rattle about imagined walks
in the park yesterday, shopping
trips she'll make next week.
A carer comes to tuck her in,
brings weak tea and egg sandwiches,
asks if I'd like some,
is relieved when I decline.
I get up to leave and the frail old cripple
who used to be my mother
says quietly: 'I always knew
what a little whore you were,'
before she spills her tea and demands
to know when cousin Betty intends returning
the fur coat.

CLEANSED   FRASER BRYANT

The girl crouched low to give the crab's hard shell a gentle tap. The critter sprang to life immediately, punching both menacing pincers high in the air. She laughed and shrieked with excitement as the creature hastily retreated to the ocean, chasing and mimicking its footwork as it did so. The bay was quiet in the late afternoon and the beach fully deserted, a silence only broken by the silky break of a wave, or the small pebbles crunching between her toes.

It had been her grandfather's present, and the girl had long wondered whether she'd ever find a place better. She loved the cove for everything it didn't have. There were no glass fragments lined with cheap liquor, no handwritten notes among the sands, not a single trace of deceit in the fresh breeze. Even the colossal sea was itself an unexpected comfort. She'd peer across the masses of water, devising a city of marble pillars and colourful fish deep below. *Perhaps I could join them*, thought the girl, *perhaps it's even more beautiful than here.*

So pretty it was to her, she barely noticed as the earth began to shake.

First the pebbles scattered as if aroused by flame, then the palms strained and twisted in their roots. The girl lost her balance falling backwards as her head collided with the rocky floor, rows of teeth smashing into one another. Even the sky ripped apart as she shielded her eyes and covered her ears with her hands.

And then it was over. Before she was back on her knees the bay had returned to its tranquil state. The trees relaxed and casually leaned over the waters, the sun shone just as it always had done, and the panicked crabs returned to their business. The girl slowly crawled to the edge of the ocean. When she looked this time, there was no fantasy in her mind.

Father, Mother, Grandpa...

With a burst of energy she darted up the dusty track towards her family's café. Climbing the steps of the veranda entrance, she found her father indoors: five cards in one hand, the other wrapped around some petroleum-like concoction.

'Papa! Did you not feel it?'

The men at the table turned to face the girl, but her father held his eyes fixed upon his cards. The room swirled thick with smoke, dominated by the scent of sweat and ash.

'Not now, Lia.'

'But Papa! Where is Mama?'

'She's just like her mother that one!' He slammed his fist on the table and smashed a cluster of gambling chips across the room, 'never knowing when to shut up or when she isn't wanted.'

Confused and afraid, the girl retreated to safety and forced herself not to weep. There was no time. *Where is Mama?* Taking a deep breath, she sprinted over the rocky terrain following the path to her grandpa's house.

The house was much larger than her parents' crudely constructed home, with tall flourishing hedges surrounding the premises. She placed her palm against the wooden gate, gasped from exhaustion, and pushed. Her mother's laughter overwhelmed her immediately, as did her uncle's chuckle. The two relaxed below her grandfather's shady gazebo, a glass in each hand.

'Lia!' Her mother dropped her drink in shock. 'Lia, what are you...?'

'I thought Grandpa would be here.' The girl stood frozen in place, as her stare shifted to her uncle.

'Oh Lia...' Her mother's startled expression soon caved to a warm sympathetic smile. 'I'm so sorry, sweetheart, Grandpa passed away peacefully in his sleep last night. The doctor said he felt no pain.' She approached her daughter gently and smothered her in her arms. 'It's OK, sweetness, you're here now. Your uncle's going to take care of us all. Don't worry, my darling, everything's going to be OK.'

This time the girl did cry; even her mother's embrace was void of any warmth or affection. Her uncle watched on from behind and offered an assuring nod. There was no one else.

She knew where it was, the place, her grandfather had taken her there the day they'd first explored the cove. 'On the southern tip of the island you'll find a steep staircase, leading higher than any other. Up here you'll always be safe, up here there'll be no one to look down on you.' She recalled his words.

'Mama, did you not hear the ground shake?'

'What, darling?' Her mother's attention had already returned to the uncle. 'Oh sorry, sweetness, I've no time for games today, let's play tomorrow OK?'

With that the girl turned, and hesitated, before continuing her walk away from the house. She followed the path from memory, hurrying her way across the island as she passed half-naked adults drinking and dancing in the sun, herds of people gathered around two bloodied roosters, and endless music blasted through the summer heat.

Finally she reached the base, and craned her neck upwards. The stone stairway climbed at an unnerving gradient, twisting its way through the trees and protruding boulders of the high peak. She crouched on all fours and felt each step one at a time, just as he'd shown her.

At the summit, the island became a painted landscape of emeralds, clear blues, and sparkling shades of gold. The girl leaned against the wooden railings, watching a lizard hastily run over the top to join her. She closed her eyes, and remembered what he'd said that day.

'When I was younger, I would come up here to view the glorious and breath-taking wonders our island has to offer. But now whenever I gaze, Lia, the beauty I once saw is contaminated. Tainted with lust, impaired with violence, corrupted with sin.

Sometimes a generation arrives which should never bounce forwards. You can be kind, and you can be loving, but there are times when your children would be better dropped in the ocean. For fear you might give life to a liar, married to a coward, lusting for a thief, and an innocent girl who I fear will be unjustly cleansed with the rest of them.'

Suddenly the tides all around her began to withdraw, as the ocean drew breath.

'When the earth breaks apart, Lia, promise me you'll come up here.'

The sun was falling now, and the girl pictured the sea's critters scuttering up the shore towards land. Lia took hold of the lizard, planted a kiss, and spun round and round in a playful dance. The island fell quiet, as the waters softly rumbled in the distance.

IN THE KASBAH   MARIA ISAKOVA BENNETT

they eat sliced oranges
bright with sugar.

He pours mint tea from a height,
loves the drama.

She's in his darkness.
A purple shadow makes a thumb print,
a smudge, a small mistake.

It's a squall of white that captures her attention,
alters something,

like the promise of a covenant.
She could speak
or take the lemons from this scrubbed table,

but she doesn't want to disturb
the arrangement.

AFTERIMAGE / OBLIVIOUS OF THE BIRDS
DARACH BRADISH

Cliffs of Moher, photographed 1910
Four people are seated at a round table.

See

Here is the photograph,
    an outing captured
        in the still

pools of shadow,
    and the stacks of cliff,
        chairs, table, seated ladies,

nothing shifting
    on the wide bare ledge.

Fading distances, and
    rounds of greyness settling
        into afterimage.

Imagine;
    soundscapes crack
        open the Atlantic grumble,

wind-lofted voices sail,
    rise and fall and rise
        to tumble yet again

to a breathless halt.

The snap man called the shot.
  One shutter slap,
    generations after seeing

only still-life holding in
  of swollen lungs,
    captor and captive

waiting to exhale an ocean,
  oblivious of the birds.

Biographical Details

Daragh Bradish's poems have appeared widely in Ireland, the UK and Europe in journals such as *Crannóg, Revival, The Moth, Poetry Salzburg Review, The French Literary Review*, and *Orbis*. His first collection *Easter in March* was published in 2016 by Liberties Press.

Fraser Bryant is based in London. He is a regular writer and reader for the Bovine Cemetery fiction evenings held in Brighton, and is currently working on his first fantasy novel in addition to his short stories.

Patrick Chapman's books include two volumes of stories and seven poetry collections, the latest of which is *Slow Clocks of Decay* (Salmon, 2016). He is co-editor of the poetry magazine *The Pickled Body*. He has also written an award-winning short film and many episodes of children's animated television. His audio credits include writing a *Doctor Who* adventure, and producing B7's award-winning dramatisation of Ray Bradbury's *The Martian Chronicles* for BBC Radio 4, starring Derek Jacobi and Hayley Atwell.

Louise G. Cole was longlisted in the Dermot Healy Poetry Competition, 2015, and placed third in the Strokestown Poetry Festival Prize in 2015 and 2016. She performs her poetry at the Word Corner Café in the Dock Arts Centre, Carrick-on-Shannon, and at pop-up shows in the west of Ireland with the Hermit Collective, a wandering band of writers, artists and musicians. She was nominated for a Hennessy Literary Award in fiction in 2015. https://louisegcolewriter.wordpress.com

Bernie Crawford is on the editorial team of *Skylight 47*. She won first prize in The Dead Good Poetry Competition in 2013. She has been longlisted and shortlisted for a number of competitions including Over the Edge, Fish Poetry, and Poems for Patience. She has been invited to read at a number of venues including Clifden Arts Festival, Lady Gregory Autumn Gathering, Erris Festival of Literature. Her poems have appeared in several publications.

John Davies has had work published in *Rosebud, Orbis, The Pedestal, Killing The Angel, QU Literary Magazine, The Interpreter's House* and *Smoke*.

Gerald Dawe's most recent collections are *Selected Poems* (2012) and *Mickey Finn's Air* (2014).

Ann Egan has held residencies in counties, hospitals, schools, secure residencies and prisons. Her books are: *Landing the Sea* (Bradshaw Books), *The Wren Women* (Black Mountain Press), *Brigit of Kildare* (Kildare Library and Arts Services) and *Telling Time* (Bradshaw Books). She has edited more than twenty books, including *The Midlands Arts and Culture Review, 2010*.

Frank Farrelly's poems have appeared in *Crannóg, The SHOp, The Stinging Fly, The Moth, The Fish Anthology, Poets Meet Politics, Boyne Berries, The Stony Thursday Book, Revival*, and *The Honest Ulsterman*. He was runner-up in The Doolin Poetry Prize 2015.

Chloe Firetto-Toomey is an English-American poet-essayist pursuing an MFA at Florida International University. She is the author of *Beyond Gravity*, a collection of poems published in 2001 by Loebertas Publishing. Her poems and essays have appeared, or are forthcoming, in *Crab Fat, Arsenic Lobster, Crack The Spine, Cosmonauts Avenue, Origins*, and elsewhere. She is also an editor of *Gulf Stream* and *PANK* literary magazines.

Sharon Frame Gay grew up a child of the highway, playing by the side of the road. She is an internationally published author, with works in several anthologies as well as *Gravel Magazine, Fiction on the Web, Literally Stories, Literary Orphans, Fabula Argentea, Halcyon Days* and others. She is a Pushcart Prize nominee.

D.G. Geis' first book, *Mockumentary*, is forthcoming from Tupelo Press (Leapfolio) in 2017. Most recently his poetry has appeared, or is forthcoming, in *Fjords, Skylight 47, Memoryhouse, The Fish Anthology* and *The Naugatuck Review*. He will be featured in a forthcoming Tupelo Press chapbook anthologising nine New Poets. He is winner of *Blue Bonnet Review*'s Fall 2015 Poetry Contest and a finalist for both The New Alchemy and Fish Prizes. He is editor-at-large of *Tamsen*.

Kevin Graham's poems have appeared in various journals. A chapbook will appear shortly from Smithereens Press. He is working on a first collection.

Donal Hayes is a writer and radio documentary maker living in Kinsale, Co. Cork. He has broadcast on RTÉ, CBC and C103. His writing has been published in the *Irish Examiner, The Irish Times, Literary Orphans, Newer York*, and online.

Rachael Hegarty is widely published in national and international journals and has broadcast on RTÉ Radio 1. She has won the Francis Ledwidge Prize and has been shortlisted for the Hennessey New Irish Writer and Forward Poetry Prizes. Her debut collection, *Flight Paths Over Finglas*, about which Paula Meehan, the former Ireland Professor of Poetry, said 'This poet, from a poem-rich place, makes me feel poetry is in good hands', will be published by Salmon in 2017.

Maria Isakova Bennett's pamphlet, *Caveat*, was published in 2015. She won the Ver Open Poetry Competition in 2014. She regularly writes reviews for *Orbis*. Her poetry has been published widely including work in *Southword, Envoi, Manchester Review, Tears in the Fence, Bare Fiction, Crannóg, The Interpreter's House* and in anthologies by *Cinnamon Press* and *Eyewear*. She works for charities in Liverpool as a poet and artist.

Niall Keegan is editor at The National Archives, Kew. Formerly he was assistant editor at Dalkey Archive Press, Dublin. He holds an MA in Anglo-Irish Literature & Drama from University College, Dublin.

Sarah Kelly is from Sligo and is currently in her third year of the BA with Creative Writing degree at NUI Galway. She has previously been published in *Ropes*.

Seán Kenny is the winner of a Hennessy Literary Award and was named Over The Edge New Writer of the Year. His stories have appeared in Over the Edge and Hennessy anthologies, *Crannóg, The Irish Times, The South Circular* and *Southword* in addition to being broadcast on RTÉ Radio One.

Noel King has had poems, haiku and short stories published in magazines and journals in thirty-eight countries. His poetry collections, all published by Salmon, are *Prophesying the Past* (2010), *The Stern Wave* (2013) and *Sons* (2015). He has edited over fifty books for Doghouse Books between 2003 and 2013 and was poetry editor of *Revival Literary Journal* (Limerick Writers' Centre) in 2012/13. A short story collection, *The Key Signature & Other Stories* will be published by Liberties Press in 2017.

Adrienne Leavy is originally from Dundalk but has lived in Phoenix, Arizona for many years. Her poems have appeared in *A Modest Review, Boyne Berries, Crannóg, Revival* and *The Stony Thursday Book*. She is the editor and publisher of *Reading Ireland: The Little Magazine*, a digital journal which promotes Irish literature and contemporary Irish writing: www.readingireland.net She is also the literary chair of the Phoenix/Ennis Sister Cities Book Festival.

Miles Lowry is a Canadian sound and visual artist, writer and director best known for his life-size sculptures and fragments which explore the body as an emotive, expressive canvas. His sculptural installation, *DISSOLVE/REVEAL*, portraying a group of iron figures appearing to disintegrate, was chosen as Peoples Choice at Vancouver's Artropolis 2002 and he was subsequently a subject for CBC television's Artspots, shown nationally. A solo exhibition, *RITES AND PASSAGES*, followed his interest in cultures both ancient and modern and was mounted at the Simon Fraser Gallery in 2004. His ongoing series of cast sculptural figures, *Crucial Fragments*, have established him as one of Western Canada's most versatile contemporary artists. He is continuing to explore dance and media through writing, directing and designing for live performance, television, video and multi-media collaboration as an Artistic Co-Director for Suddenly Dance Theatre in Victoria. His cinematic poem, *Opium*, based on French poet Jean Cocteau, was produced for Canadian television and selected for the 2007 Dance on Camera Festival at The Lincoln Centre in New York City. Two short films, *Aisling*, a homage to Irish independence by Liam McUistin, and *Guthrie Swims the Lake*, a poetic montage of Irish theatre director Tyrone Guthrie, have been completed for Bravo FACT! television. His latest book is *Blood Orange: The Paul Bowles Poems*, a biography in verse from Ekstasis Editions 2008 and forthcoming is *Saint Cloud – Cocteau, Cinema and the Cure*, due this spring. As a painter he has recently presented *Marks of Devotion*, an exploration of painting and calligraphy with Georgia Angelopolous, and *Saints of Circumstance*, a collection of cryptic portraits in paper, wood, wax and pigment. He is creating an ongoing collection of works based on travel and sanctuary and specifically his residencies at the Tyrone Guthrie Centre at Annaghmakerrig in Ireland. A self-trained artist, his works are seen in a wide variety of exhibitions, publications and performances. An online venue to purchase his photographs and other publications, www.loveandliberty.ca, has recently opened. www.mileslowry.ca

Eamonn Lynskey's poetry has appeared widely in magazines and journals, including previously in *Crannóg*. He has published two collections, *Dispatches & Recollections* (Lapwing, 1998) and *And Suddenly the Sun Again* (Seven Towers, 2010). www.eamonnlynskey.com

Aoibheann McCann has published short fiction in several national and international literary magazines including previously in *Crannóg*. She has had stories included in the anthologies *No Love Lost* and *The Body I Live In*, published by Pankhearst Press, UK. Her story *Johnny Claire* was shortlisted for a WOW! Award, 2015.

Clare McCotter won the IHS Dóchas Ireland Haiku Award 2010 and 2011. In 2013 she won The British Tanka Award. She judged the British Haiku Award 2011 and 2012. She has published numerous peer-reviewed articles on Belfast born Beatrice Grimshaw's travel writing and fiction. Her poetry has appeared in *Abridged, Boyne Berries, The Cannon's Mouth, Crannóg, Cyphers, Decanto, Envoi, The Galway Review, The Honest Ulsterman, Iota, Irish Feminist Review, The Leaf Book Anthology 2008, The Linnet's Wings, The Moth, A New Ulster, The Poetry Bus* (forthcoming), *Poetry24, Reflexion, Revival, The SHOp, The Stony Thursday Book* and *The Stinging Fly. Black Horse Running*, her first collection of haiku, tanka and haibun, was published in 2012.

Simone Martel's debut novel, *A Cat Came Back*, will be published in December by Harvard Square Editions. She is also the author of a memoir, *The Expectant Gardener*, and a story collection, *Exile's Garden*. After studying English at U.C. Berkeley, she operated an organic tomato farm and she is working on a new novel based on that experience.

Sara Mullen's work has previously appeared in *Burning Bush 2* and *A Thoroughly Good Blue*. She received her M.Phil. in Creative Writing from The Oscar Wilde Centre, Trinity College, Dublin.

John Murphy's debut collection, *The Book Of Water*, was published in 2012 by Salmon Poetry. His second collection, *The Language Hospital*, is forthcoming from Salmon in September 2016. He has been three times shortlisted for the Bridport Prize (Prize winner 2013), and three times shortlisted for the Hennessy Cognac/*Irish Times* writing awards. He was shortlisted for the 2016 UK National Poetry Competition. He is a two-time winner of the Strokestown International Poetry Prize (2015, 2016). His poems have been published in many journals and magazines, including *Cyphers, AMBIT, Mimesis, Stony Thursday Book*, and *Poetry Ireland Review*.

David Morgan O'Connor contributes monthly to *The Review Review* and *New Pages*. His writing has appeared in *Barcelona Metropolitan, Collective Exiles, Across the Margin, Headland, Cecile's Writers, Bohemia, Beechwood, Fiction, After the Pause, The Great American Lit Mag* (Pushcart nomination), *The New Quarterly* and *The Guardian*. He is fiction editor of *The Blue Mesa Review*. @dmoconnorwrites.

Mary O'Donnell is a poet, novelist and short-story writer. Her most recent collection of poems is *Those April Fevers* (Arc Publications, UK), and her most recent novel is *Where They Lie* (New Island Books). She worked as an Adjunct Professor for Carlow University Pittsburgh's MFA in creative writing for eleven years.

James O'Sullivan has been published in numerous literary journals and anthologies, including *The SHOp, Southword, Cyphers*, and *Revival*. He was placed third in the Gregory O'Donoghue International Poetry Prize, 2016 and was commended in both the Munster Literature Centre's Fool for Poetry 2014 International Chapbook Competition and the Charles Macklin Poetry Prize 2013. He has twice been shortlisted for the Fish Poetry Prize, as well as the Fish Short Story Prize 2014/15. His third collection of poetry, *Courting Katie*, is forthcoming from Salmon Poetry in 2017. He has also published numerous works of visual art and photography. He is the founding editor of New Binary Press. http://josullivan.org.

Cheryl Pearson's poetry has appeared in publications including *Compass Magazine, The Journal*, and *Skylark Review* (Little Lantern Press). She has had a poem featured in *The Guardian*'s Poetry Workshop feature, and was shortlisted for the York Literature Festival Poetry Prize, and the Princemere Poetry Prize 2015. She was placed third in *Bare Fiction* magazine's 2016 poetry competition. She has work in the forthcoming issues of *Envoi, Interpreter's House*, and *Neon Magazine*. She is currently working on her first full-length poetry collection.

Matt Prater's work has appeared in a number of journals, including *The Honest Ulsterman* and *The Moth*. He is MFA candidate in poetry at Virginia Tech in the USA.

Liz Quirke's poetry has appeared in various publications, including *New Irish Writing* in *The Irish Times* and *The Best New British and Irish Poets 2016* (Eyewear Publishing). She was shortlisted in the Emerging Poetry category of the 45th Hennessy Literary Awards.

C. R. Resetarits has new fiction out now in *Best Short Stories* from *The Saturday Evening Post Great American Fiction Contest 2016, The Chicago Quarterly Review*, and *Midwestern Gothic*; out soon in *The Southwest Review, The Wisconsin Review*, and *Stand*. Her poetry collection, *Brood*, was recently published by Mongrel Empire Press, 2015.

Rosemarie Rowley has written extensively in form: *Flight into Reality* (1989, reprinted 2010) is an extended original work in terza rima. She has four times won the Epic award in the Scottish International Open Poetry Competition. Her books include *The Sea of Affliction* (1987), the first ecofeminist work. Her most recent book is *Girls of the Globe* (Arlen House, 2015).

Michael Sharp's poetry has been published on both sides of the Atlantic, most recently on the *Honest Ulsterman* website and in *Gutter 14*. He attended the Royal Conservatoire of Scotland and the University of Wisconsin-Madison.

Knute Skinner's collection, *The Other Shoe*, won the 2004-2005 Pavement Saw Chapbook Award. His most recent collection, *Fifty Years: Poems 1957-2007*, from Salmon Poetry, contains new work collected along with work taken from thirteen previous books. A memoir, *Help Me to a Getaway*, was published by Salmon in March 2010. www.knuteskinner.com

Michael G. Smith's poetry has been published or is forthcoming in *Borderlands: Texas Poetry Review, Cider Press Review, Nimrod, Sin Fronteras, Sulphur River Literary Review, The Santa Fe Literary Review*, and other journals and anthologies. *The Dark is Different in Reverse* was published by Bitterzoet Press in 2013. *No Small Things* was published by Tres Chicas Books in 2014. *The Dippers Do Their Part*, a collaboration with visual artist Laura Young of haibun and katagami from their Shotpouch Cabin residency, was published by Miriam's Well in 2015.

Anne Tannam's work has appeared in literary journals in Ireland and abroad including *Poetry Ireland Review, The Moth, Poetry Bus, Burning Bush, Skylight47, Bare Hands Poetry, Irish Literary Review* and *Prairie Schooner*. Her first book of poetry, *Take This Life*, was published by Wordsonthestreet in 2011, and her second will be published by Salmon Poetry in 2017.

Rosamund Taylor was shortlisted for the Montreal International Poetry Prize for the second time in 2015 and was also a runner-up for the Patrick Kavanagh Award that year. She has been published in *Agenda, Magma, Orbis* and *The Stony Thursday Book*. Her poem, *Between Cupar and Kirkcaldy,* which appeared in *Crannóg 37*, was nominated for a Pushcart Prize.

Steve Wade was a prize nominee for the PEN/O'Henry Award, 2011, and a prize nominee for the Pushcart Prize, 2013. His novel *On Hikers' Hill* was awarded first prize in the UK abook2read Literary Competition, December 2010. Among the publications in which is work appears are: *Crannóg, Boyne Berries, Zenfri Publications, New Fables, Gem Street, Grey Sparrow, Fjords Arts and Literary Review*, and *Aesthetica Creative Works Annual*, 2011 and 2015. www.stephenwade.ie

Eamonn Wall is a native of Co. Wexford but has lived in the US since 1982. Recent publications include two edited volumes of James Liddy's essays for Arlen House and *Junction City: New and Selected Poems 1990–2015*, Salmon Poetry.

Stay in touch with Crannóg
@
www.crannogmagazine.com

Lightning Source UK Ltd.
Milton Keynes UK
UKOW02f0237280916

283933UK00002B/52/P